JORDAN MURRAY

BEST-SELLING AUTHOR

THE CLEARING

A SUSPENSE THRILLER

ISBN-13: 978-1-7771060-5-8

The Clearing

First printed July 2023

Cover design by Jordan Murray via Book Cover Zone

Interior design and formatting by Jordan Murray

Editing by Claire Macaulay

1   2   3   4   5   6   7   8   9   10

also by
Jordan Murray

The Carlson Case – a companion novella to The Clearing (coming

soon)

The Clearing (2023)

I Did It for You (2022)

Bird Boy: and Other Short Stories (2020)

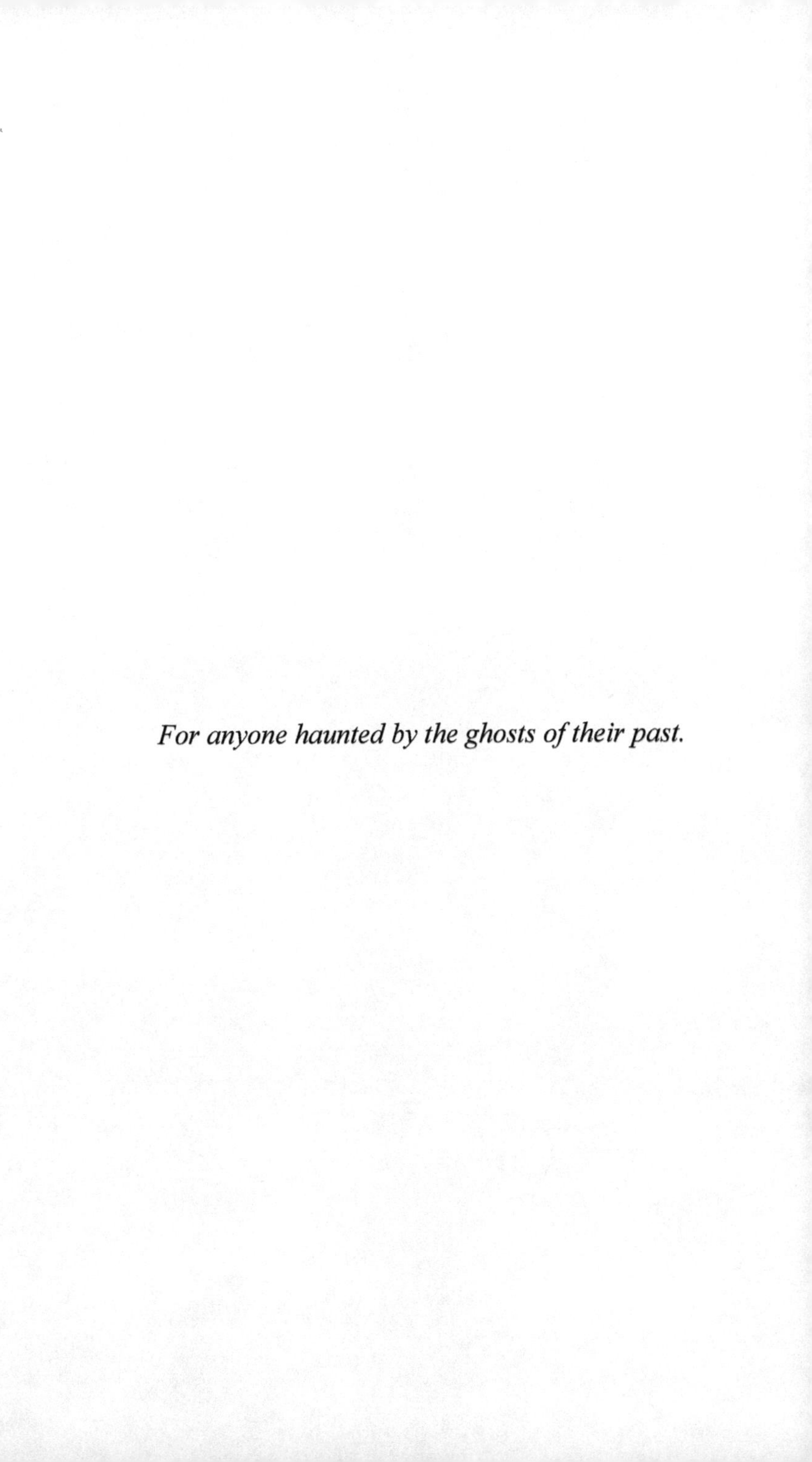

For anyone haunted by the ghosts of their past.

Prologue

The Carlson Family

2017

The haunting had woven its tendrils through the fabric of the Carlson household, every nook and cranny plagued by an insidious spectre; according to Mr. Emmanuel Carlson, at least.

Doors slammed by themselves, the sound reverberating through the walls. Cold spots materialized in specific areas of the house, chilling the air and causing the hairs on his arms to perpetually stand on end. Picture frames toppled over and books fell from shelves, pushed by invisible hands. And the voices – sinister whispers that toed the edge of audibility – seemed to speak directly into Emmanuel Carlson's tortured ears, a malevolence only he was privy to.

Mr. Carlson, whom the spirits seemed to exclusively burden, suffered under the weight of the supernatural beings. They followed him around every corner. His wife, Linda, and their children, Brian, Todd, and Charlotte, heard and saw nothing. They experienced none of what Emmanuel did, and this phenomenon continued for weeks.

The rest of the Carlson clan grew concerned for the family patriarch. With each passing minute, Emmanuel was becoming more tense by the supernatural events plaguing their home. When little Charlotte was a week away from her sixth birthday, Linda Carlson suggested they hold a small birthday gathering at the Carlson house.

"Under no circumstance," Emmanuel thundered, his words echoing through the house, "shall anyone ever step foot inside our home until we have rid ourselves of these demons!"

Beads of perspiration formed on Emmanuel's forehead, glistening under the harsh kitchen light, as his hands clenched into tight fists. His eyes darted anxiously around the room as if they were being watched by someone – or something.

Uncharacteristic of his typically composed demeanour, Emmanuel's voice cracked, betraying his fear. It was a sight his wife had never seen, a revelation that left her wide-eyed and silent, her heart aching for the man she loved.

"I thought they were ghosts," retorted Brian, the ever-skeptical eldest Carlson child. His mischievous younger brother, Todd, giggled alongside him.

Emmanuel simply went upstairs and locked himself in his bedroom, becoming a ghost in his own right. He missed work, wouldn't eat or sleep, and was absolutely petrified of the evil spirits looming around the house. Finally, Linda Carlson decided that enough was enough; she would indulge her husband's delusions only to get rid of them, once and for all.

After hours of scouring the Internet, Linda came across a ghost-hunting group local to the area. They called themselves The Larua Group, *larua* being the Latin word for ghost, according to their homepage. Within twenty-four hours, the group had travelled to the small hamlet in which the Carlsons resided.

They brought with them trinkets and gadgets, some machines that beeped and ones that played white noise, feeding into their charade of authority. Linda knew instantly that they were phonies, but she was counting on the farce.

For the first time in what seemed like forever,

Emmanuel's eyes lit up with hope when he learned of Linda's efforts to hire the services of paranormal specialists; ones who promised to perform their trademark ritual known as a Clearing.He believed fervently that his home, and his family, would soon be safe once more.

On the rainy night of June 27th, 2017, The Larua Group performed a Clearing of all evil spirits and paranormal activity in the Carlson family house.

They commenced an elaborate spectacle, moving through their home with the practiced precision of con artists, their technological contraptions emitting a chorus of sounds. Linda watched them, her heart heavy with skepticism and hope, while Emmanuel followed their every move, captivated.

Despite the many bodies roaming the Carlson home, the space felt eerily empty to Linda without her children, who had been dropped off at her parents' house earlier that evening.

This performance, this illusion of protection, was the last lifeline Linda Carlson could offer to her husband.

After expunging the ghosts, The Larua Group went on their merry way, pockets heavy with cash, off to scam their next customer. Linda was pleased and hoped her husband would be at peace, too.

By June 30th, over half of the Carlson family would be dead.

One

Beck

2019

When I was thirteen years old, I shot my stepfather, and for twelve years it stayed a secret – until today.

Ledger, my boyfriend – ex-boyfriend now, technically – stands before me, wielding a letter that was never meant to be read in the first place. It's moments like these when my resentment towards him comes to a boil, his behaviour reminding me of my dirtbag stepfather, Randy. Yet even amidst the chaos of emotions, I can't help but feel a pang of guilt for comparing the two. Ledger may have his moments, but I still love him, despite everything he's done to hurt me.

"I thought both of your parents were dead," says Ledger, a stern expression cemented on his otherwise handsome face.

I gnaw on my lower lip before responding.

"Half of that is the truth."

"And the other half?"

I pause, calculating my next move. He's obviously read the letter, so there's no way for me to weasel out of this. I can't deny it.

Why the hell did Ledger have to find this one thing today, the day I'm moving out of his apartment?

The letter must have slipped out from the book I keep it hidden in. That, or Ledger was looking through my things as I packed up. The latter wouldn't surprise me one bit.

"The other half is in that letter," I respond.

I continue throwing my DVDs from the living room's media cabinet into my *Mr. Darcy* tote bag, determined to leave this apartment as quickly as possible. But each movie I pack away brings with it a memory of Ledger, and I'm reminded of why I love him so much. I think of the times we laughed while watching old Pixar movies, especially the one with my favourite cartoon fish. I think of the times he comforted me while I bawled my eyes out to a Nicholas Sparks movie. The times I cowered into his strong arms while watching horror movies even though I wasn't scared at all. Movies are our thing, always have been. Our DVD collection and decorative movie posters were once our pride and joy.

But that's over now, and so are we.

"That one's mine," Ledger mumbles, pointing to a DVD case in my hands.

"What?"

"*The Blind Side*. That's mine."

I look down at the case in my hands and see that he's correct, so I chuck the DVD at him like a Frisbee. Ledger doesn't bother making the catch, and it drops to the ground with a hollow rattle.

"How fitting. I sure felt blind-sided when I walked in on you and your *friend*," I scoff.

Last night, I came home from going to the movie theatre with Kinsley because a wicked rainstorm caused the building's power to go out. We were all sent home with a free movie voucher for the inconvenience, which was fine by me. To my sister's dismay, I was excited to get home to Ledger earlier than expected. She's never been that fond of him.

I dropped Kinsley off at her place before driving myself back home to Ledger and I's apartment, but when I went to unlock the door, it was already open a crack. Terrible thoughts rushed through my mind. *Was there a home invasion? Did someone break in? Was Ledger hurt?* My world was shattered when I finally mustered the courage to step inside, my car key between my knuckles, to see Ledger, balls deep, railing some nameless blonde against our kitchen counter. The sight pierced through me like a jagged shard of glass, splintering my illusions of love and trust. At that moment, I knew it was over, so I dropped my soaking wet coat and purse on the floor and walked past them into the bedroom to begin packing my bags.

"And I'm also feeling quite blind-sided by discovering that my girlfriend of two years murdered her stepfather when she was a kid," says Ledger casually.

"I didn't *murder* him, okay?" I yell, stepping towards him. Ledger doesn't flinch or move away.

"He-he was abusive," I say, my voice shaking with raw emotion. "To my mom. And to me and Kinsley."

My eyes well up with tears as I recall the haunting memories etched deep within my soul. Memories of bruised flesh and the suffocating darkness of black and blue eyes flood my mind. No matter how hard I try to bury them, they always rise to the surface again. But it wasn't just the physical wounds that scarred me.

"He hit us. He said awful things to us. We were just

kids," I add, my voice barely above a whisper as if the weight of those words alone could crush me.

Ledger's eyes soften, his features reflecting a combination of shock and remorse.

"Babe, I'm sorry. I didn't know," he confesses, his voice laced with genuine regret.

"I'm not your babe. And no, you didn't. I wanted to move past it, so I didn't tell you because I didn't want it to affect things between us. I know that doesn't excuse it at all, but I–"

"But nothing." Ledger reaches out to take my trembling hand in his. His touch, warm and reassuring, sends a shiver through my body. "Come here," he urges gently, his eyes searching mine for a glimmer of understanding. "You shouldn't have had to go through that as a kid. I'm so sorry, Becky."

Becky.

His pet name for me is a weakness I'll never overcome, and my heart, marked by its fractured state, opens up to him once more. It was never truly closed, even after his betrayal. Just because a heart is broken doesn't mean it's devoid of love. My heart, which has been a little bit broken all my life, finds solace in the presence of Ledger, the glue that binds the shattered pieces together. The realization dawns upon me, illuminating the depth of my feelings. I need him.

I collapse on the ground from the overwhelming

emotions taking over my mind and body. Ledger has always been there to catch me when I fall, no matter the circumstance, and this time is no different. He sits on the floor with me now as I rest my head on his lap and sob. And as I lay there, my head nestled in the safety of Ledger's lap, a whirlwind of conflicting emotions envelops me. My memories of his betrayal mix with this fleeting, tender moment.

The wound inflicted by his infidelity is still raw, but there's a part of me that clings to him, convinced that I need him to hold me together. Throughout the years we've been together, I found comfort and a sense of belonging. It's a familiarity that tugs at the deepest recesses of my being, whispering promises of solace and security – things I never knew growing up. Things I struggled to provide for my younger sister, Kinsley.

"I love you, Becky."

Ledger's words resonate with me, despite them being said countless times over the course of our relationship. At this moment, they carry the weight of his remorse and the sincerity of his love. He accepts the darkest parts of me, the parts even I can't bear to acknowledge. But forgiveness is a delicate dance, and although I know I need time to heal, to cope with the pain of his betrayal, I don't hesitate when I tell him I love him too.

Sometimes it's just easier to throw a bandage on a wound and call it healed.

Two

Kinsley

2019

I take a seat at our regular booth in *Smokey's Pancake House*, a locally owned diner, and wait for my sister to arrive.

The air is thick with the smell of sizzling bacon and stale coffee, scents that – over the years – seem to have seeped into every surface in the building. The walls are decorated with vintage metal signs and faded photographs of local landmarks. For as long as Beck and I have come to *Smokey's*, everything in this diner has remained the same. The signs, the pictures, the peeling faux-leather booths, all of it. It was the only place we could afford growing up, and the owner often gave us an extra pancake or two, given our situation. Everyone knew about what happened to our parents, and they pitied the Rollins sisters. Since we were practically orphaned at such a young age, Beck and I went everywhere together; did everything together. The definition of a package deal.

But today, there's only one Rollins sister. For now, at least. We agreed to meet at 9:30 am for breakfast, and now its 9:48 am, and Beck still isn't here.

Beck is almost always late, which I hate. I'm the person who shows up fifteen minutes early for an appointment, and Beck is the person who struts in five minutes late with an iced coffee and not a care in the world. Despite her lack of punctuality, she more than makes up for it with her loving personality and large heart. I wouldn't have gotten through our childhood had it not been for Beck. She practically raised me.

A flash of long, auburn hair flies by me as Beck walks by and slides into the booth across from me, the weathered seat squeaking in protest as she settles.

"Did Smokey come by yet?" Beck asks.

"Fortunately for you, he hasn't." I wink at her. "I would never dare to order before you."

Smokey is the namesake of this breakfast joint, as well as the cartoon mascot on the sign and marketing materials. The cartoon Smokey is a breakfast sausage with a beard and moustache that we liken to the owner of the place. We don't know if it was intentional or not, and we've never asked. It was Beck who first referred to Brett as Smokey, and it's stuck ever since. Smokey has become a part of our personal mythology, with a whole backstory (he's a divorced father of two) and personality. I kind of feel bad calling him that behind his back, but then again, I never did have Beck's sense of humour.

"What can I get you girls on this fine morning?" Smokey asks, his voice gruff yet friendly, carrying the weight of countless conversations held over these tables. Unlike the *Smokey's* waiters and waitresses, Smokey doesn't use a pen and pad to document the order. Since he's the one who created the menu, every ingredient of every meal is etched into his brain. It's impressive, considering the menu is four pages long and expands every year.

Beck studies the menu momentarily, her fingers tapping nervously against the laminate. "Hm, I think I'll just have a coffee, please. Black."

She closes the menu and slides it to the edge of the table.

I raise an eyebrow at my sister. She doesn't eat enough, and I know it's because her dumb ex-boyfriend made a comment about her weight last year. If you ask her though, she'll say otherwise, always wanting to protect Ledger and the way people perceive him. I'm relieved she found the strength to break free from that toxicity and kick his sorry ass to the curb, but I can't help but worry about the scars that remain.

"And an order of pancakes," she adds.

Smokey nods. When he turns to me, I push the menu towards him and recite my regular order from memory. An order of strawberry crepes with whipped cream and fresh strawberries; a glass of orange juice because, despite working at a coffee franchise, coffee makes me jittery; and a side of grits. It's our unspoken ritual.

"You know the drill; it'll be about twenty minutes for the food. I'll bring the coffee right over," Smokey says, disappearing into the kitchen.

"So," I say.

"So," she echoes.

The ambiance of the diner, with the sound of cutlery against ceramic and murmurs of fellow patrons, offers a veil of privacy amidst the din of the world. It's usually comforting as background noise to our conversations, but today, it's highlighting the awkwardness of our silence.

"How are you feeling after last night?" I inquire, trying to bridge the gap between us. "If I ever get my hands on him, I'll cut off his cheating little dick and make him live celibate for the rest of his life. Now *that* is a fate worse than death for a guy like Ledger."

Beck doesn't laugh, which is how I know something is wrong. I don't usually cuss or speak ill of anyone, and she typically thinks it's hilarious whenever I say things like 'shit'. She doesn't even try to muster a response of any kind, and that's when I make the realization. He's done it again; he's dragged Beck back down the rabbit hole that is their relationship.

"About that," Beck says timidly.

"Why? Why the hell would you get back together with him after what he did? He's a cheating scumbag and you deserve a million times better than him. I've been telling you that all along, even before he screwed some other girl."

"I know, and he feels really bad about it. We had a big talk about the whole infidelity thing last night and –"

"Uh, yeah, he should feel bad about cheating on you, but that doesn't mean that you take him back. He hurt you, Beck. I've never seen you so broken before."

After walking in on Ledger, Beck called me as she packed her bags. She was sobbing, and Beck almost never cries. I offered for her to come to stay with me, but she declined, saying she wanted to face things head-on. If I had known that meant getting back together with him the same night she dumped him, I would never have let her stay.

Smokey returns with our drink orders. Beck immediately sips the scalding hot coffee she ordered in an attempt to keep her mind occupied and her mouth shut. I don't touch my orange juice.

"I know, I'm sorry. Once we started talking, I broke down and..." Beck pauses and closes her eyes, like she's trying to remember words from a script.

"I ended up telling him some pretty personal things and I thought he'd be, well, *Ledger* about it. I half expected him to threaten to blackmail me back into the relationship or manipulate me somehow. But he didn't do any of that," Beck continues, her expression brightening. "I was at my worst, and he didn't judge me at all. Ledger accepts me and loves me for who I am, despite what I've done. It made me fall in love with him all over again, even if he hurt me. I still haven't fully forgiven him, so don't worry about that. I'm going to make him earn my forgiveness and trust again."

The happiness in my sister's eyes makes me want to shake her or slap her, or both. Why can't she see that by 'accepting' her, Ledger is manipulating her? Whatever she told him, he's going to use it against her one day, I just know it. And I might not be able to protect her from the blow-back when he does.

"Why isn't *my* unconditional love and acceptance

enough for you? Your entire life, you've been looking for some external validation of your worth. You want to be worthy of love in spite of your flaws. And you are. I've loved you since I could first utter the words as a baby. I've never stopped loving you or done anything to make you question it, have I?" I ask rhetorically. "The answer is no. And you know it."

"I know you love me, Kins," says Beck, reaching her hand across the table. I let her take my own hand into her grasp but don't squeeze back. "It's just that…it's different with Ledger. You're my sister and you've always been my sister. We're blood-related, and in my mind, you're kind of biased, I guess. Ledger's not, and he and I have only known each other for two and a half years, compared to the twenty-two years you've known me."

Smokey comes by with a platter of pancakes and a plate of crepes, and drops them on the table, bobbing his head along to whatever music he has playing in his earbuds.

"So, my acceptance doesn't mean anything because I'm biased," I quip. "Okay, yeah. I see how it is."

Without breaking eye contact with Beck, I stab my fork into a strawberry and begin eating while Beck sits across from me like a statue.

Beck and I rarely fight, our bond nearly unbreakable even when we face challenges. But ever since Ledger entered her life, a quiet yet undeniable shift has occurred, leaving me feeling helpless and unsure of my role in her life. The worst part is that she doesn't even realize it.

"You know that's not what I meant," she mumbles.

"No, I don't."

We eat our breakfast in silence until Beck makes a request.

"I know now isn't the best time, but I have a favour to ask," Beck says. "Alison quit. She ended up getting a position in marketing in Alberta and left earlier this week. It was a last-minute thing, Alison didn't give us any notice, and we had no time to find a replacement. I wouldn't ask, but we have a job tonight and we need someone else who knows the operations side of things to fill her position. It would just be temporary. Please, you'd be doing me a huge favour."

"First you tell me you're back together with Ledger, and now you tell me you're still in this stupid group, and that you want me in it, too? No. I quit for a reason. I didn't like what we were doing, but no one seemed to care what I thought. All anyone cared about was the money."

Beck's eyes search mine, pleading for understanding. "I know, and I'm sorry. But I wouldn't ask if I didn't have any other option. Please, Kinsley, you know I need this money."

I stop chewing, my fork hovering mid-air, and let out a loud sigh.

"You're lucky I love you," I say, half-jokingly.

And she is.

Three

Beck & Kinsley

2006

Birthdays were not celebrated with particular importance in the Rollins household. Beck's thirteenth birthday was no exception.

The air in their small, cramped living room felt heavy and suffocating as if even the walls were complicit to Randy's strict rules. The only visitors welcomed within those walls were Randy's poker buddies, their raucous laughter and smoke-laden breaths lingering in the air like a reminder of Beck's isolation. One year, Randy held a poker tournament on Beck's birthday.

Beck was used to it, though. She had learned to expect the desolation that accompanied her date of birth and navigate Randy's regime.

Her younger sister, Kinsley, was not yet acclimated.

Wide-eyed and innocent, Kinsley was the very definition of a social butterfly, flitting from one friend's birthday party to another. The absence of her own birthday party weighed on her heart and crushed her spirits. Kinsley did not fully comprehend why she was denied the same simple pleasure experienced by all her classmates. Despite her lack of understanding, Kinsley never fussed. She did what she was told and never questioned Randy's rules, even if it concerned her lifelong dream of having a real celebration.

Beck expected her thirteenth birthday to be like any other, marked by a family dinner and perhaps a present or two to bookend the evening. There would be no decorations or cake or singing of Happy Birthday. There never was. To Beck's surprise, her mother had put up a few streamers in the doorway to the dining room in an attempt to decorate, but they were faded and weathered. Beck appreciated them nonetheless, though, because her mother had never taken such a risk before.

Beck, Kinsley, their mother, and Randy sat down at the table for the Rollins special – TV dinners. Plastic trays containing TV dinners were plopped unceremoniously on the table. As the birthday girl, Beck was granted the privilege of getting the first pick of her microwaved feast, settling for macaroni and cheese. Disappointment clouded her expression as she took the first bite. The lack of cheesiness in the mac and cheese was a stark reminder of the absence of indulgence on her special day. A desiccated brownie sat untouched next to the mediocre meal, its dryness matching the parched expanse of the Sahara Desert.

"Well, it's your birthday, Rebecca," Randy declared. "Only five more to go until you're eighteen and out of the house."

Beck and Kinsley's mom laughed along awkwardly. Kinsley sat still in her chair, not recognizing the implication of Randy's comment.

"Happy birthday, sweetie," Beck's mother said.

"Happ-bird-day, Beck," Kinsley added.

"God damn it, Kinsley, don't talk with food in your mouth!" Randy yelled.

The plates on the table shook when his fist met with the table's surface, the scent of alcohol emanated from his mouth. As instructed, Kinsley finished chewing her food and repeated her birthday wish to her sister, albeit with much less enthusiasm.

"Thank you." Beck's voice quivered, and the family continued eating in silence.

"I have a surprise for you, sweetie."

Beck's mother got up and opened the fridge door.

Oh my gosh, Beck had thought. *Am I actually getting… a birthday cake?*

Beck finished her food quickly, with the exception of the dry brownie, eager to taste her first-ever birthday cake. She crossed her fingers and hoped that her mom got her favourite flavour, chocolate. Although any flavour at all would do, really. Beggars can't be choosers, after all – as Randy so often likes to remind his girls. But Beck's face sulked when her mother brought out a rhubarb pie, instead.

"A birthday…pie?" Beck asked, with a hint of sass. More sarcastic comments danced on her lips, but Beck knew better than to make 'smart-ass' remarks.

"It was on sale, and I know how much everyone likes pie," Beck's mother explained, trying to smile. Her smile faltered every few seconds, revealing her true feelings about the dreaded birthday pie, but she would quickly recover with an even wider grin.

Beck's face soured. She knew that the real reason for her birthday pie was that Randy liked the dessert better than cake. And if they were going to get anything for her birthday, of course, it would be catered to him.

Stupid Randy, she thought.

"Oh, you shouldn't have," Randy joked. "But give me a

piece, anyway."

As her mother served Randy a generous slice, Beck and Kinsley waited at the table, Beck's anticipation mingling with disappointment. The first bite of the pie confirmed her worst fears – the lacklustre taste further intensified her defeat. Each chew felt like an echo of the countless disappointments they had endured.

"I just can't take it anymore!!"

For a moment, Beck wondered if she had accidentally spoken her thoughts aloud. That is, until Beck's mother stood up and giddily ran out of the room. The remaining Rollins family members sat in silence until she reappeared, thrusting a present into Beck's grasp.

"I can't wait any longer. You have to open it now." Beck had never seen her mother so excited about a present before, namely because there were so few presents in the first place.

Beck's own excitement was double her mother's when she lifted the lid to the box to reveal a vibrant blue ukulele. Beck had been learning the ukulele at school in music class and had taken to the instrument fondly. It was even her act in the talent show that her family didn't come to, but she'd had to borrow one of the school's ukes for the performance.

Beck's gratitude overflowed as she leaped from her seat, enveloping her mother in a tight embrace.

"Thank you thank you thank you!"

As Beck strung a chord, the weight of her mundane life was lifted by the sound of music. Along with her present, Beck's mother's warm embrace had made her mediocre birthday into a great one.

Beck and her mother synchronously whipped their heads in Randy's direction as the sound of splintering wood and snapping strings reverberated through the room.

"And how much was this piece of shit? Too much, that's what I say."

"Randy, don't swear like that in front of the girls."

Beck's mother attempted to intervene; her voice strained with a plea for civility. Yet, the tension in the room escalated, the feeling palpable even to Kinsley.

"Then don't fucking disobey the budget we have in place. There's a procedure here, Barb. You buy some expensive gift for one, you have to get it for the other, too." Randy spoke of his stepdaughters with contempt, not bothering to mention them by name.

Beck's parents continued to argue, but she quickly blocked it out. Her focus was directed toward the broken ukulele on the ground, the neck snapped right off the body. The gift had been taken away from her before she could even strum the strings. She would never feel the vibrations of the notes when her fingers plucked away on the frets of that elusive, baby-blue ukulele. Her eyes welled up with tears, dripping onto the ukulele, staining its wood with her shattered hopes.

Kinsley closed her eyes. She hated it when her parents argued. Beck wanted to leave the table but could not, as she had not been dismissed. Eventually, Beck squeezed her eyes shut, too. As the dispute continued, the cacophony of their parents' voices merged with the harsh sound of flesh meeting flesh – a sharp slap followed by a yelp. Beck's eyes shot open, and her heart sank. *Screw the rules*, Beck thought. She hastily retreated upstairs; each step punctuated by the echoes of insults and yelling. Kinsley, sensing the distress, followed her sister into their shared bedroom. They sought refuge in the confined space, huddled together on Beck's bed, pillows clutched tightly against their ears, attempting to drown out the painful noises below.

***

The next morning, Beck stirred from her slumber to find Kinsley missing from her bed. *The little bugger,* Beck sleepily thought. Beck and Kinsley usually waited for each other before going downstairs for breakfast, but Kinsley must have gone ahead without her.

Suppressing a yawn, Beck swung her legs over the edge

of the bed, stretching her tired limbs. She looked around her bedroom until her gaze fell upon the desk that stood across from her, where the shattered ukulele lay. Beck thought it odd, as she did not remember anyone bringing it into her room the previous night. It was a bittersweet sight, a testament to both her mother's unwavering love and defiance, as well as Beck's broken dreams. Upon closer inspection, the ukulele was not unchanged. Something caught Beck's attention; it was not quite as broken as it had been the night before.

Duct tape crisscrossed the instrument's body, holding the fractured pieces together with makeshift mending. Each of the four strings had been messily restrung and looked to be on the verge of breaking once more. It was a crude repair, far from perfect, but Beck smiled. Kinsley had tried to fix the ukulele and left a scribbled note that read:

Im Sorry your guitar
droke. I trieb fixin it
for you. Love Kinsley

Beck's gaze lingered on the patched-up ukulele, her fingers tracing the rough edges of the tape. She knew that the ukulele would never produce the melodies she had once dreamed of. Beck would never take it to music class or perform with it at next year's talent show. But it held a different kind of beauty – a testament to the love that Kinsley poured into every haphazardly placed strip of tape.

***

It was not 24 hours later that Randy spotted the artfully repaired ukulele from the upstairs hallway and tossed it out with the trash to be picked up by the morning garbage collection.

Four

Beck

2019

I drive back home following my disastrous breakfast with Kinsley.

I feel awful about making her upset, but she has to understand that Ledger makes me happy. Yes, he's hurt me, but that's what humans do. We make mistakes and we learn from those mistakes. And if you truly love someone, you'll love every inch of their being, despite their flaws and mistakes, but also because of them. It sounds corny, like something from one of those romance movies Kinsley and I love to watch, but that's how Ledger and I love each other. No matter how mad we get or what bad thing we do, we're magnets, always being pulled back together.

Kinsley is such a good person and I'm proud to call her my sister and best friend; I just wish that she'd accept Ledger as part of the family. Their first interaction at a dinner I planned for the three of us left a sour taste in Kinsley's mouth, branding Ledger as a smart-ass. It's an assessment not far from the truth, and oddly enough, it's that very quality that draws me to him. As a fellow smart-ass, I find his wit endearing. Things were fine between them as long as they stayed in their own lanes, but when Kinsley learned about The Larua Group, things spiralled into a mess we have yet to untangle, two years later.

The job we have tonight sounds simple enough from the briefing Ledger left for me on the kitchen table this morning. An older woman is convinced her deceased husband is haunting her townhouse, where she lives alone. These cases, the ones involving elderly people, are the ones that upset me the most. None of what we do is good or morally permissible, but capitalizing on the emotional and psychological vulnerability of an older person just feels… wrong. The money we get from it, though? The money we earn is undeniably alluring. It tugs at me, whispering that it's worth it, that it aligns with my dreams and ambitions.

After graduating with a Bachelor of Arts degree in social sciences two years ago, I've been saving up to get my Master's in psychology. But it's expensive as hell, and I'm set on attending the best university in Toronto, which is extremely competitive and financially crippling. I have a lot of hurdles to overcome before I'm even ready to apply, the largest being my finances. The school's hefty price tag threatens to shatter my aspirations, but it's my dream university, and I'll relentlessly do whatever I can to earn the funds to attend.

To make ends meet, I toil away as a freelance writer, juggling a wide range of projects—editing, proofreading, and scriptwriting. The pay is unpredictable, often a rollercoaster ride. However, my involvement with The Larua Group offers increased stability and a chance to pad my pockets with extra cash. I'll grapple with being morally ambiguous because I know that this gray area is the bridge to my ultimate goal – a fulfilling career as a psychologist or therapist.

The inception of The Larua Group was Ledger's brainchild, an idea that came to him in the shower in 2017, shortly after I met him. Ledger confessed he had a childhood fascination with the supernatural, and the thought of roleplaying as ghost hunters for cash amused him. He rounded up his closest friends and me, and we embarked on a test run that surpassed his expectations. The Larua Group proved to be a convincing act, earning us a couple of hundred bucks for less than an hour's work. Since then, we've honed our techniques, invested in new equipment, and assigned designated roles to each member to make things run more smoothly. Our aim was to increase believability and enhance the appearance of legitimacy, ensuring our clients got an experience they would never forget.

Ledger exudes a natural aura of confidence and swagger that demands attention and respect, making him the undoubtable leader of the group. His role extends far beyond that though, as he takes on the responsibility of scouting potential hauntings and, when appropriate, engaging in dialogue with homeowners to captivate their interest. One time, he convinced a man at a bar to hire The Larua Group as a prank for a Halloween party to scare his friends, and we did just that. Ledger is a people-person, and that comes in handy when hot or cold pitching for jobs. Ledger also handles the logistical aspects of our cases, meticulously organizing travel, accommodations, and various other details that ensure smooth operations.

Brooklyn, Ledger's older sister by four years, has a knack for transforming us into a professional and polished team.

Aesthetically, that is. She effortlessly emanates a sense of elegance and sophistication, always dressed in designer outfits and flawlessly applied makeup. When I first started dating Ledger, I used to envy Brooklyn's impeccable fashion sense, feeling inadequate in my worn-out sneakers and ripped jeans compared to her gold earrings and stiletto high heels. But Brooklyn's ability to make us look the part of genuine ghost hunters, if such a thing even exists, both repels and fascinates me in equal measure.

For each investigation, Brooklyn carefully selects attire that strikes a balance between professionalism and the eerie nature of our work. She artfully combines elements of classic sophistication with subtle hints of darkness, creating a distinctive ensemble for each team member that complements their individual personalities. When it comes to my own wardrobe, Brooklyn takes into account my preference for comfort and practicality. For Ledger, she emphasizes his charisma by choosing tailored dress shirts that exude confidence and authority. The choice of dark, rich colours adds an air of mystery and intrigue, perfectly aligning with the enigmatic nature of our ghostly pursuits. To reflect our friend, Sam's, tech-savvy persona, Brooklyn incorporates subtle nods to his passion for innovation. For a few of our cases, she's chosen a shirt with discreet patterns reminiscent of circuitry or incorporates accessories that showcase his love for technology. Sam is the one behind the devices, and his wardrobe is a visual reminder of his expertise.

Sam is Ledger's friend from college. He's our resident tech genius and helps operate all our ghost-hunting equipment. He also helped engineer our own equipment to help with the credibility of our investigations and clearings, such as a Larua-branded EMF sensor and a Ghost Box. Like me, Sam has a day job. He works at some bigwig tech company in the city, but only for a few days of the week. The job doubles as a cover so that Sam's fiancé, Toby, doesn't find out about our side hustle.

From what Sam's told me, I've gathered that Toby and Kinsley have similar core values; family, truth, and morality. And, knowing how Kinsley feels about our work, I can only imagine that Toby would have a similar reaction, if not a worse one. Kinsley is my sister, but Toby is Sam's fiancé. Maybe I'm wrong, but I think lying to your fiancé about how you're paying the bills is much worse.

Kinsley was once a vital member of The Larua Group, primarily handling the financial aspects of our jobs. She took charge of payouts, managing travel expenses, and all other monetary responsibilities. With the exception of Sam, who's practically family anyway, our group was a family business. The Larua Five. But the nature of our work became too much for

Kinsley to bear, and she left. Kinsley always was the better of us Rollins sisters, in nearly every way imaginable, but especially morally. After her departure, we reluctantly filled her position with Alison, a friend of Brooklyn's, who proved competent but could never truly replace Kinsley, an original member. Alison was all right at what she did, but nothing beat the original Larua Five.

With Kinsley's return to the fold for a few select jobs, and with my goal of earning enough money for my Master's degree within reach, I'm filled with an overwhelming sense of excitement.

Things can only go up from here.

***

"He's here, I know it. I just know it."

Mrs. Gadot, our newest employer, is in hysterics when we arrive on the front steps of her decrepit townhouse. We hadn't even fully made it to the porch when the door swung open, and an older woman sped out to greet us.

She's holding a golden picture frame in her trembling hands, with a photograph of a young man in a soldier's uniform encased within it.

"This is him, my husband, Phil," she exclaims, pointing at the picture.

I look over my shoulder at Kinsley, who is standing behind everyone else. She looks extremely uncomfortable, but Ledger, with his natural charm, effortlessly diffuses the initial awkwardness between us and the distressed homeowner.

"That's a lovely picture, Mrs. Gadot. May we please come inside to discuss Phil some more? I'd love to hear more about him."

Ledger smiles warmly, his smooth voice and even tone immediately calming Mrs. Gadot's erratic behaviour. Ledger tends to have that effect on people.

"Of course, of course. And please, call me Gladys."

We all funnel inside the house, and the smell of potpourri hits me like a brick, assaulting my nostrils. The petite old lady bounces around on hobbled footsteps and motions for us to sit down. Everyone complies but Sam, who is occupied bringing in our equipment from the van.

"So, Gladys," Ledger begins, "can you tell us a bit about what's been going on in your home? Why do you believe that your husband is haunting you, and not at peace in heaven?"

"It started a few months ago, right after my Phillip passed on." Mrs. Gadot presses her lips on the picture frame for a quick kiss and makes the sign of the cross before continuing.

"The first night alone, I just couldn't fall asleep for the life of me. I got up around midnight and decided to get a snack, maybe a box of raisins or some crackers. I can't remember which. When I went into the kitchen, though, there he was, sitting in his armchair, doing a crossword. And then like that, he was gone. Poof!"

Sam's body jolts at the loudness of the *Poof*! and I try not to giggle.

Ledger, who's sitting next to me, is pretending to write notes on a little notepad. In actuality, he's drawing a famous cartoon dog.

"And please, correct me if I say something inaccurate, Gladys," says Ledger. "But we're here to confirm that this spirit is, in fact, Phil? Is that right?"

"Yes, that's correct. In my heart, I know it's him, but I need proof for my children. They think I'm as nutty as a chocolate bar. Sometimes I think they might shove me in a home, ha!"

"Thank you for sharing your story with us, Mrs. Gadot," I say, softly. "Where do most of these occurrences take place? Is there a certain room or area in your house that Phil likes to frequent?"

"Well, I always see him sitting in his armchair, right over there," Mrs. Gadot replies, pointing a shaky finger toward

Kinsley, who's occupying an old recliner. Suddenly aware of the seat's significance, Kinsley promptly vacates the chair, probably feeling guilty about impeding on the old man's favourite spot.

Brooklyn stands up next, approaching Mrs. Gadot. "If it's okay with you, Gladys, we're going to start setting up our equipment around the room."

"Yes, yes, of course! Don't let an old broad like me get in your way." Mrs. Gadot takes an exaggerated step back, and we begin.

Sam skilfully begins the set-up of some cameras around the room, securing them in tripods and positioning one to face Mr. Gadot's suede recliner. Ledger helps Brooklyn set up the EMF detector since she refuses to harm her acrylic nails, while I untangle the chords to our motion detectors. Kinsley stands awkwardly in the corner, staring at everyone with an uneasy expression. Her body is rigid in a way I've never seen before.

After noticing Kinsley's demeanour, Sam beckons me over to where he's fidgeting with an EMF detector.

"How do I put this nicely," Sam muses. "Kinsley is throwing a major wrench in this job. She's acting like an amateur; like she's never done this before. I know it's her first case back and all, but she's being awkward. Maybe go give her a sisterly talk and warm her up a bit?"

Mrs. Gadot hobbles by, peering over to witness the setup. Sam and I smile and nod politely as she moves on to Ledger's side of the room.

"Okay, I'll try,"

"Good. Thanks. I can't afford to lose out on the payout from this job," Sam whispers.

I raise my eyebrow.

"I'm saving up for a new desktop and gaming keyboard," he elaborates. "The switches on my current keyboard just aren't doing it for me anymore."

"I have no idea what that means, but I'll talk to Kinsley, don't worry. You'll get your computer and the right switch-things."

Leaving Sam, I return to my original post and call Kinsley over. "Hey, Kins, can you help me with these chords?"

Once Kinsley's made her way over to me, I whisper, "You're giving off some weird vibes. We don't want Mrs. Gadot to think there's something off."

"There *is* something off," Kinsley whispers intensely. "This whole thing is off, and you know it. I left the group for a reason. The only reason I'm doing this right now is for you."

The furrow in her brow and slight trembling of her lower lip makes it seem as if she feels bad for the attitude. But I know that it's true. I hate that she's doing this for me. I hate how that fact makes me feel.

"I know, and I appreciate it. I appreciate *you*."

"And I appreciate you," says Ledger, appearing behind me. He sneaks a kiss on my cheek, and Kinsley shoots him a disapproving look. Ledger isn't fazed by her reaction and does it again to bug her. I wish Kinsley would just get along with him. Ledger likes to play around, but he doesn't have any problem with my sister. The feeling isn't mutual, though. Ledger and I are together, and that's not going to change. Kinsley just needs to get over it.

"Aw, you're the sweetest," I coo, my voice laced with affection. Ledger gives my hand a squeeze and returns to the EMF detector. Kinsley makes a sour face at me as if she might vomit. *She can be so immature sometimes.* I scoff at her as we finish untangling the wires, and I decide it's time for Kinsley to have a job of her own.

"Kinsley, maybe you and Mrs. Gadot could grab us some more drinks before we get started," I say, making sure my voice projects authority.

"More drinks, of course! Let's go, dear, and grab you and your friends some refreshments," Mrs. Gadot says excitedly. Kinsley walks silently into the kitchen with Mrs. Gadot, and the second they're out of view, I seize the opportunity and get to work.

I wander around the cramped room, weaving around

cameras and furniture, examining and assessing everything I can while we have the space to ourselves. The wall adjacent to the sofa is full of framed photographs, and I view each one closely. It looks as if Mrs. Gadot has two children, a boy and a girl, each of them now grown with families of their own. There's a photo of a slightly younger Mr. Gadot in a hospital, receiving what looks to be chemotherapy in a stark white hospital room. Mrs. Gadot is in the corner of the photo holding his hand. The bookcase nearby is filled with worn copies of medicinal books and doctoral training textbooks. I run my fingers along the spines as I read the titles and continue looking around the room until I hear two pairs of footsteps approaching. I rush back to my previous spot near the motion sensors. I hope this is enough to get by on.

"Delivery!" Mrs. Gadot sings, appearing from the kitchen alongside Kinsley. We all rise and grab a glass of lemonade from the platter Mrs. Gadot and Kinsley are balancing. I take a sip and try to hide the contortion of my face. It tastes like pure lemon and salt.

"Delicious," I remark.

"Thank you, dear."

"All right, Gladys," says Ledger. "We're all set up, so I think we'll get started if that's okay with you."

Mrs. Gadot agrees, and the show begins.

Sam turns off the lights, explaining that it's better to have them off to connect to the other side, and gives Ledger a subtle nod. Ledger turns on the devices, one by one, and takes a seat on an ottoman facing the recliner.

"Phil," he says. "Phillip Gadot, are you here? If you're here, please give us a sign. Give your wife, Gladys, a sign that you're with us."

Nothing happens, and I step forward to play my part.

"Phil, my name is Beck. Mrs. Gadot – Gladys – says that you like to sit in this chair," I say, gesturing to the recliner. "Is it all right if I take a seat in your chair?"

The EMF detector goes off with a ping, 'indicating' a spiritual presence. Mrs. Gadot jumps from the noise but settles herself quickly. My eyes dart over to Sam, who's holding the remote that controls the phony EMF detector.

"Okay, Phil. I'm going to take a seat now and ask you a few questions." I sit down, and after settling and looking around the room, I conjure a blank expression on my face. I stare forward intensely, not focusing on anything or anyone in particular. My vision becomes blurry.

"What's wrong with her?" Mrs. Gadot asks in a loud whisper.

Ledger leans over and whispers, "She's our resident clairvoyant. Beck can see visions, and she feels things." But I can't, and I don't. "Beck can connect with people on the other side. It takes a toll on her emotionally, but she's just compelled to help people. It's her calling, her vocation."

I smile at him, shyly tucking a piece of auburn hair behind my ear. Vocation is a bit extreme, but I have to roll with it.

"Gladys?" I ask. "Phil is here, right now, in this chair. I can feel his energy pulsing through my veins." I take a deliberate, deep breath, inhaling the air that hangs heavy with Mrs. Gadot's emotions, and exhale slowly. The room is still and charged with anticipation as I break the silence.

"Phil had been sick for a while, and he'd beat his cancer. Overcome it. He was a strong man, a pillar of the beautiful family you'd built together. The love he held for you and your children was boundless, and that's why his own suffering pained him so deeply. It wasn't his own pain that saddened him; it was the thought of his family going through their own pain because of his illness. Phil had an extraordinary selflessness that was sometimes challenging for you to witness, is that right, Mrs. Gadot?" She nods, tears welling in her eyes. "There were many times that you wished he'd take care of himself. For once, you just wanted him to put himself first."

Mrs. Gadot whispers softly, her voice filled with sadness, "If only he hadn't smoked all those years… He wouldn't have gotten so ill if he wasn't a smoker. Phil always teased that he was too stubborn to get sick, too tough for cancer to claim him."

"He did have that funny sense of humour to him, didn't he?" I ask with fondness.

From across the space, I meet Mrs. Gadot's gaze, her eyes filled with a mixture of anticipation and sadness. Sadness flickers within me, and for the first time since we've arrived, I acknowledge that I truly feel bad for this poor old woman. I shove the thoughts out of my mind while I continue my act.

"Now, Mrs. Gadot, I'm going to ask Phil directly why he's here, in your home."

I close my eyes and tilt my head upwards, opening my body up to become a conduit, a vessel for spirit communication. That's what it looks like, at least. Palpable silence fills the room once more, so quiet that I can hear Kinsley's breath catch at the suddenness of which I open my eyes and meet Mrs. Gadot's from across the room.

"Phil, is there anything you'd like Gladys to know? Any final words you wish to say to your wife?"

The EMF detector goes off once again, and a distinct ping rings through the room. I paint a serious yet thoughtful expression on my face as I turn to look at Mrs. Gadot.

"Phil says that he loves you and that he wants to say

goodbye. He understands that you two were never afforded the opportunity for a proper goodbye," I say gently.

Overwhelmed by the raw emotions spilling out from within her, Mrs. Gadot collapses to her knees. Ledger moves swiftly to catch her, mirroring the support he had extended to me when he found the letter I'd written to my mother. The room fills with the raw intensity of Mrs. Gadot's cries as if her very soul is unfurling. The sight of this elderly, fragile woman succumbing to such profound emotions leaves us all frozen, unsure of how to ease her pain or continue from here.

"Oh, Phil. Oh, oh!" Another sob escapes her. "I love you, too. I love you."

Ledger helps Mrs. Gadot to her feet and guides her to the couch, where he sits next to her. I wait a moment, hoping Ledger's presence will soothe her enough that we can move on to the final step of The Clearing.

"Mrs. Gadot, Phil is just about ready to pass on to the afterlife now. You can take this opportunity to say your final goodbye. Remember, even though Phil has departed physically, his soul will always reside in your memories and linger in the realm of spirit."

As Mrs. Gadot retains Phil's picture frame and says a heartbreaking goodbye, everyone is silent. Time suspends itself as Mrs. Gadot clings to the picture frame, her trembling hands a testament to the profound love and longing she feels for her deceased husband. Each word she utters in her heartbreaking farewell echoes through the room, enveloping us in the palpable weight of her sorrow; but not all of us. As Mrs. Gadot pours her heart out to a room of strangers, an array of emotions permeates the room. Ledger's demeanour remains unaffected, the epitome of stoic strength amidst the tide of emotions. Brooklyn's disinterest manifests as unmistakable boredom, her attention drifting elsewhere. Sam's face portrays a blend of seriousness and inscrutability, his emotions carefully guarded so that he doesn't feel too much. Amidst this tableau, I notice Kinsley backing out of the room, her eyes red and glistening with unshed tears. Of course, the first job she comes back to is one of the most emotional cases we've ever done.

I offer her a gentle nod from across the room, aware of the toll this work has on her mentally and emotionally. I allow her to leave the emotionally charged room, but I cannot allow her to leave The Larua Group. With Alison gone and no permanent replacement in sight, Kinsley remains an indispensable member of our team.

After another five, ten, or maybe thirty minutes, Mrs. Gadot finishes her final goodbye. Kinsley is gone from the hallway when we start to clear out the room, probably at home already, wrapped up in a blanket. Hiding from her feelings and the world, no doubt. Over the years, I've done my best to shield her from the harsh realities of our world, and that includes hiding the truth about what happened to Randy all those years ago. But we're adults now, and as much as I want to protect her from anything with the potential to cause her pain – including The Larua Group – I can't.

Like me, she'll just have to deal with it.

Five

Kinsley

2019

After we finish the job at the Gadot house, I stumble back to my cramped apartment, the weight of the day clinging to my skin like dried-on dirt.

As I enter the shower, I desperately try to scrub the guilt off me. The scalding water falling from the showerhead offers little comfort, and every droplet that cascades over my body becomes an attempt to wash away the darkness that lingers. But no matter how hard I scrub; I cannot erase the dirty feelings stemming from my actions today. I shouldn't have agreed to rejoin the group, even if it was just temporarily. The allure of helping my sister clouded my judgment, blurring the line between right and wrong.

Mrs. Gadot's kindness remains etched in my memory, a painful reminder of the trust she placed in a group of strangers. She opened her heart and home to us, believing that we could bring her closure. But instead, we preyed upon her; we took advantage of a grieving old woman. Mrs. Gadot's husband is not haunting her townhouse, and it's obvious that she's conjured these hallucinations to cope with losing the love of her life. We knew that before we even stepped foot on her property or met the woman. But that's what we do. The Larua Group hunts ghosts; they clear spaces of spirits and spectres, anything otherworldly. they also clear their client's pocketbooks in the process.

Standing in the cascade of water, I cry.

I cry until my tears blend into the shower droplets and I can't tell them apart.

Ghosts aren't real, but the ones that live within us are. They haunt us in everything we do.

Beck and I know that all too well.

Six

Beck

2019

When Ledger and I return to our apartment, we do so in a silence that hangs heavy between us, thick with the unspoken acknowledgement of what we have just accomplished.

Once we're inside, Ledger places his wallet and the envelope of money on the kitchen counter before realizing his mistake. I want to take a sledgehammer to that countertop.

We move to the wooden dining room table instead, its

surface bearing the marks of countless cases discussed made and secrets shared. Ledger rips open the envelope and pours the money onto the table.

One and a half hours of our time translates into a substantial sum of $4,500 with an additional $250 tip, which testifies to the nature of our work. Each member of The Larua Group, me included, will walk away with nearly $1000 cash. Unlike most of our other jobs, the Gadot case magnifies the nature of what it is that we're doing. We always teeter on the line between right and wrong, but in such an emotionally charged case with a frail, innocent woman, our willingness to do so makes me feel dirty. I try to rationalize my involvement, justifying it as another step towards securing my future. Each $100 bill represents another building block toward my degree and career; a career where I'll help people and make up for all of the bad things I've done in my life, including the Gadot case.

Including Randy.

As Ledger hands me my stack of bills, I grasp onto the hope that once I hold that certificate in my hands, the guilt associated with these cases will dissipate like a fading memory.

I change into my pyjamas and curl up next to Ledger on the couch, seeking familiarity to distract me from the shame I feel.

In the safety of Ledger's presence, I find solace in the

unspoken love and understanding that he grants me. The letter I wrote has been acknowledged but intentionally shelved for now. He knows that I need some time to myself before I'm ready to tell him everything, and he respects that. Ledger recognizes the balance I try so hard to maintain, living with the knowledge of my crime and lying about it to protect both me and my sister.

Ledger puts on a movie for us, one of the action films he loves to watch, and the light from the TV screen dimly illuminates the dark room. I try to watch but can't stop thinking about the letter and its contents.

I've never fully processed what happened with Randy and my mom, mostly because I don't want to; I just can't. It's a kind of self-imposed amnesia, a protective shield I've created to protect myself from the past. Yet, even in my present life as an adult, I bear the weight of that night's consequences, reminders that the choice I made irrevocably altered the course of my family's lives. The scars of our past may be hidden, but their influence on our lives remains a constant, haunting refrain.

I was thirteen years old when *it* happened, but I was only six or seven when I witnessed my mother's ill-fated marriage to Randy. When they married, we moved into Randy's bungalow, which was a luxurious upgrade from the dingy rental apartment where the three of us previously resided. That was perhaps the only positive gained from the relationship, but that home was turned into a battlefield where the clench of his fists and the sting of his blows marked the rhythm of our new lives. Initially, he stayed away from Kinsley, recognizing that she was only a freckled, wide-eyed toddler. My mother and I did not have the same luxury.

Randy's wrath knew no bounds, his aggression fueled by the poison of alcohol coursing through his veins. He drank every morning and every night, and in retrospect, I can hardly believe he didn't die of alcohol poisoning or liver failure. But eventually, Kinsley matured and was no longer protected by her youthful innocence. She grew up and subsequently grew into Randy's alcohol-fueled routine of slaps, punches, and belt beatings.

"Beck?" Ledger's voice cuts through my reverie.

"Huh?" I say, confused.

"I asked if you wanted popcorn. I'll just grab a big bowl to share."

Ledger chuckles as he stands up, his hand affectionately tousling the top of my head before he heads toward the kitchen. I admire his dark brown hair from the couch and wonder what our children would look like.

They'd be beautiful babies regardless of whose hair colour they inherit, as brown and auburn have their own unique allure. Although Ledger did mention once that he didn't like 'ginger babies' because he thought they looked like the fictional doll from his least favourite horror franchise. Maybe brown hair would be best then.

Ledger and I both have green eyes, so our children would undoubtedly have them, too. I'm filled with warmth at the mere thought of wide green eyes staring at me, begging me to read a bedtime story or go to the park. Would they inherit my wit and penchant for sarcasm, or would they adopt Ledger's more serious and stoic nature? Perhaps they'll have a mixture of both, a testament to our unique relationship. And we'll definitely have family movie nights in the home theatre that Ledger and I dream about building in our future home.

Growing up, the luxury of family movie nights and trips to the theatre was foreign to us. Most of our mother's limited income as a part-time receptionist was siphoned away by Randy's insatiable thirst for alcohol, his *booze fund*, as he liked to call it. There was little room left over for her own indulgences, let alone ours. But with Ledger by my side, I know I can give our children the childhood I was robbed of. The contrast between my previous life and the one within my grasp overwhelms me with a surge of anticipation.

Before Ledger found out the truth, I lived day-by-day for a reason, because tomorrow wasn't guaranteed. It's something my mother always said. Every day felt like a tightrope walk where my secrets threatened to shatter the life that I'd built for myself. The looming dread of the police coming to apprehend me for my past misdeeds has haunted me for over a decade; it's my shadow, concealed in the dark but never fully dissipating. And even worse, I've harboured similar anxiety that Kinsley would discover who really pulled the trigger that night and never forgive me. Nothing, not even my relationship with my sister, is guaranteed.

But now, one thing in my life *is* guaranteed, and that's Ledger. The assurance of our shared future, including marriage and the prospect of children, excites me in a way I didn't know was possible. I've never let myself think this far ahead, never allowed myself to dream and plan so big. As a man, Ledger is so much better than Randy, the only male role model I had as a child. Yes, he'd strayed from our relationship, inflicting pain that pierced me deeply, but I've come to realize that the blame cannot rest solely on his shoulders. Ledger must have felt alone or unappreciated in our relationship, so he sought momentary validation from someone else. He doesn't love this woman; she was just a warm body to fill the void I'd created. So, I've promised to invest more effort in showing my love for him, recognizing that our relationship requires consistent understanding and nurturing from both of us.

Ledger returns, breaking me out of my thoughts once more, cradling a steaming bowl of buttered popcorn and our beverages. I smile at the warmth of his kiss against my forehead as he sets our snacks on the coffee table before us. He's thoughtfully brought a refreshing glass of water for me and a can of pop for himself.

"Was there only one can of pop left?"

Ledger shakes his head. "I just think that you should probably drink more water. You drink pop all the time, and those drinks are packed with sugar, fat, and a lot of other unhealthy stuff. You want to be thin and healthy, don't you?"

I nod, grateful for his consideration.

"Of course, I do. Thanks."

He leans in, planting a light kiss on my lips, and I can't help but smile.

Ledger's always looking out for me, even when I'm not looking out for myself.

He's good like that.

Seven

Kinsley

2019

TWO MONTHS LATER

Still smelling like espresso and stale donuts, I come home from a graveyard shift at the 24-hour coffee shop where I work.

My pug, Chester, waddles to the front door to greet me

with doggie kisses. Despite being exhausted, I scoop him up and smother him with love.

As much as I don't want to do the Larua jobs, I won't deny that the extra money is good, especially when I work such a crappy job with equally crappy hours. But I hate myself for taking the money we scam people out of in the first place. Beck still hasn't found a permanent replacement for the position I'm filling, but I suspect that it's an intentional choice on her part. She doesn't want me to leave. There's been nothing but silence surrounding my exit from the group, and I've been waiting for Beck to address it – but she hasn't.

The face of my clock reads 7:00 am., and even though I should get some sleep, I decide to check my email instead. I place Chester on his dog bed and head to my desk. I frown when I see that my inbox is empty, closing my laptop in defeat.

With Chester loyally trailing behind me, I head into my bedroom and close the black-out curtains so that I can change. I remove my frustratingly brown uniform and throw each article of clothing in the corner. In its place, I slip into a silky nightdress with a cherry pattern on it. Just because I'm going to sleep doesn't mean I can't do it in comfort and in style. Once I'm finally under the covers and put my head on the pillow, my phone *pings*. Serotonin rushes through my body as I jolt out of bed and snatch my phone from on top of the dresser. But instead of an awaited email, I see a notification for a text from Ledger to the 'Larua Group-Chat.' He was really proud of himself for coming up with that one.

I'm already up and out of bed, so I begrudgingly open the message. What the hell could he want so early in the morning? I add his disregard for the sleep of other human beings to my list of reasons of why I hate Ledger. Another few messages come in immediately after opening the text and it takes me a few read-throughs to view them with confidence.

LEDGER: Hey guys. Got a new job to run by you all. It's a crazy one.

LEDGER: Can everyone come over to my place at 8:00 pm? We'll chat then.

SAM: sorry i can't. toby and i are going to go to dinner

BROOKLYN: wtf are you assholes texting about at 7 in the morning. go the hell to bed.

ME: I'm with Brooklyn on this one.

BROOKLYN: knew you would be ;)

LEDGER: Just bring Toby, Sam.

SAM: bring him to your place where we talk about our next gig, yeah great idea

SAM: sorry, no can do :/

LEDGER: This is really important, guys. Seriously. This is one of the biggest things that could happen to The Larua Group EVER. I'm talking about a big job with a big payout $$$$!!!

SAM: …. i'll see what i can do

LEDGER: Yes! That's what I like to hear. What about you, my favourite sister?

BROOKLYN: seriously guys go tf to sleep. i'll be there. i guess. muting you now, byeeeee

LEDGER: All right. We have me and Beck, Sam and Brooklyn. Kinsley, are you in?

I refuse to answer Ledger, who has the nerve of messaging us all so early in the morning, but I already know what my answer is going to be.

Like Brooklyn, I mute the chat notifications and go to bed with a faint smile on my face.

***

I wake up around noon and drag my groggy self out of bed. Chester follows close behind.

The first thing I do is check my email, but once again, it's empty aside from unwelcome junk mail and spam messages from scammers about liposuction or contest prizes. I grab some water, have a snack, and head back into my bedroom to get ready for the day. Or, whatever's left of it, at least. Losing out on half of your day is one of the many downsides of working the night shift.

I rummage through my cramped closet and decide on a floral romper that brings out the green in my eyes. As I curl my short hair in the mirror, it strikes me once again how similar, yet different Beck and I are. Apart from the length and texture of our hair – mine a tousled bob, Beck's cascading in long waves – we could easily pass as twins, despite the three-year age gap between us. When we were younger, we loved to mimic each other and dress as identically as we could. It was a game of sorts, and we almost always won. Hypothetically, we could pull a stunt like that again now, in our twenties. There's just one problem: no matter how similar our appearances may become, the moment either of us opens our mouth, the ruse unravels. Beck lives and breathes sarcasm, while others view me as naïve. Beck's intelligence and thirst for knowledge highlight one of our largest differences, as I struggled with dyslexia growing up and hated going to school.

I don't remember much about Randy, our stepdad, other than the fact that he was abusive towards us. Beck remembers more but has never wanted to talk about it, probably to protect me from the harsh reality of our childhood. So she says.

I do remember every detail of one incident, though. Randy had thrust a newspaper in front of my face as an act of cruelty, knowing full well my difficulties with reading, even before my formal diagnosis. Each time I stumbled over a word or made a mistake, Randy snatched the paper away and erupted into laughter. He'd tell me I was dumb as a rock and that I'd go nowhere in life. It was a twisted form of entertainment for him, a sick game that forever soured the way I view reading. Today, even if my dyslexia were to magically disappear, the damage Randy caused would linger.

Back then, most schools lacked the resources to support children with learning disabilities, but I was lucky to have a compassionate teacher who became my guiding light. With Mrs.

Garcia's help, I gradually gained the tools and confidence to confront my dyslexia head-on, making the task of reading less daunting. I still grapple with the occasional challenge, because dyslexia never truly disappears. Every day, following my post-work nap, I make it a point to read a page or two of the local newspaper, a small act of tribute to the younger version of myself, striving to overcome the odds.

Today's newspaper is relatively boring, so I decide to look at the advertisements at the back of the paper. I almost spit out my orange juice when I see a compact listing for The Larua Group in the classified section.

"Clearing spirits, spectres, and the supernatural since 2017", the posting reads.

The advertisement looks like satire, and I'm reminded of why I left the group in the first place. The deception, the act of swindling innocent people for our own gain… none of it sits right with me. My stomach churns at the thought of Mrs. Gadot and all of the other unsuspecting clients of The Larua Group.

I take a deep breath and remind myself that I'll only be here for one more job, and then I'm done, once and for all.

Eight

Beck & Kinsley

2006

"Isn't she just a doll?"

Kinsley despised it when her stepdad, Randy, fussed over her in front of his friends. Randy was allowed to have friends over, but Kinsley and Beck were not granted the luxury. This inequality saddened Kinsley: she did not think it was fair but never dared to say anything about it. Like her sister before her, Kinsley eventually learned to keep her mouth shut when it came to just about anything in front of Randy. Meanwhile, Beck, who had recently entered her teenage years, had found her voice and started pushing back against Randy. It was a change that Kinsley knew would bring trouble for everyone involved.

"Adorable," remarked a large man. Kinsley had never seen a man so big and could not help but stare.

"A little munchkin," agreed a short fellow.

"You'll have trouble with the boys knocking on her door in a few years."

Kinsley began to back away. She did not know what they were saying but she had heard the word 'boys'. *I hate boys, they're mean and gross*, thought Kinsley. Based on a single word, Kinsley did not want anything to do with the conversation, not comprehending the full extent of their remarks.

"And where do you think you're going, huh? Get over here." Randy playfully gestured towards Kinsley, but there was a sternness in his eyes. Kinsley did as she was told.

"That's my girl. Are you going to show Mr. Stan, Mr. Jason, and Abe how good your reading is?"

"Hey, why don't I get to be called Mr.?" asked the man called Abe. He made a funny face when he said this.

"Because you're a dirty dog who won't settle down.

Definitely not Mr. Material. But then again, neither am I!"

All the men broke into laughter, disregarding the young girl's presence and innocence. Kinsley retreated into her turtle shell, which was really an oversized hand-me-down hoodie, and tried to hide.

"Well, how about it?"

Randy's request hovered in the air, and Kinsley's eyes welled up with tears. Summoning every inch of her strength, Kinsley swallowed the lump in her throat and willed the tears to recede, refusing to let them see the light of day. Randy would not see her cry.

Randy shoved the most recent addition of the local newspaper into her dainty hands and pointed to the front page with his stubby sausage finger.

"Read it until I say stop, okay?" Kinsley had known her stepdad meant business.

Randy smiled but Kinsley did not. Such was the dynamic in the Rollins household, where smiles were scarce and often hollow, particularly when it came to Beck and Kinsley's mother. Kinsley noticed as if her mom never smiled anymore, not truly. Her mother's mouth would smile but her eyes would not.

Kinsley clutched the newspaper tightly, her hands trembling with a mixture of anxiety and dread. She knew that reading in front of Randy and his friends was a test she was bound to fail. Randy was counting on it. The act of reading had always been Kinsley's adversary, and whenever she tried to read, the words transformed into an incomprehensible jumble. Taking a shaky breath, Kinsley tried her best to focus on the words before her. As she attempted to decipher the letters and form coherent sentences, her dyslexia – at that point, undiagnosed – unleashed its familiar tricks. The words seemed to dance on the page, letters rearranging themselves and taunting her with their elusive meanings.

Her voice quivered as she stumbled over the first sentence, her eyes darting between the letters, desperately seeking clarity and stillness. The room fell into an uncomfortable silence, broken only by Randy's laugh. The sound had cut through Kinsley's heart like a sharp blade, but she was anticipating as much.

"Try again, Kinsley," Randy sneered, his voice dripping with condescension. "We all know how smart you are, don't we? So, show these intelligent men, show them what you're made of."

Kinsley tried again, but her attempts became increasingly strained and fraught with errors. Each mistake was met with laughter from Randy and his friends, their amusement growing with every faltering word. Despite her effort to present a strong front, Kinsley broke down into tears.

"I ca-can't do it, I'm sorry," Kinsley had cried.

"Whatever, just get out of here," Randy spat. "You wasted everyone's time and embarrassed me in front of my friends. Go to your room and think about that. Remember how useless you are."

Randy's words rung true, and his remarks became a ghost that would haunt Kinsley for years to come.

Nine

Beck

2019

My head throbs as I stare at a screen full of sentences that lack grammatical correctness, structure – and if I'm being honest, an ounce of coherence. With a slight shake of my head, I close the document, feeling a pang of disappointment for the client who'll have to face the harsh truth of his shortcomings as a playwriter.

I leave my laptop on my desk and head to the dining

room table to see how the preparations for tonight are coming along. A spread of appetizers, snacks, and wine decorates the table's surface, artfully arranged, and organized by colour. In the center, Ledger placed a charcuterie board with cheese and crackers. The whole arrangement looks like a culinary masterpiece ripped straight from the pages of a magazine.

"How does it look?" Ledger asks.

I gesture dramatically to the spread. "Um, how do you think it looks? It's stunning, Ledger. You did an amazing job."

I lean in and give him a kiss.

"I can only imagine what it would look like if I were the one in charge of the food," I say. Ledger chuckles.

"Beck, I love you, but I wouldn't trust you to cook anything other than soup or a microwaved meal."

The mention of microwaved meals brings me back to my childhood, when no one in our house cooked. Without his gourmet meals, I'd likely forget to feed myself. It's one of the perks of dating a chef.

At 7:59 pm, Sam and his fiancé, Toby, make their entrance. Sam is the epitome of punctuality, outshining even my perfectionist sister, Kinsley, who arrives shortly after. As Kinsley wheels her pink cruiser bike into the entryway, her pudgy pug, Chester, sits in the front basket. Kinsley retrieves the dog, and I see that Chester is wearing a snug, orange sweater. My first thought is that he looks like a pumpkin, but Kinsley would kill me if I ever spoke ill of her fur baby. Nestling her bicycle against the entryway closet, Kinsley enters the living room, cradling the small dog in her arms. Ever since Kinsley adopted Chester last year, the senior dog has become an extension of her. She refuses to go anywhere without him if she can help it.

Physical activity is an alien concept to Kinsley; she doesn't even like going up and down the stairs in her apartment building, which is so old that it lacks an elevator. A part of me believes that her inclination for bike riding is not solely for the vintage aesthetic; the retro cruiser bicycle garners her a lot of attention and compliments wherever she goes. Although she's one of my favourite people in the world, Kinsley cares too much about how she's perceived by others.

Observing Kinsley's entrance with her bicycle, Ledger arches an eyebrow from across the kitchen island. A tired expression forms upon his face, his typical response to Kinsley bringing the bicycle inside. Despite knowing that her bike never leaves the entryway, Ledger is shocked and annoyed each time Kinsley visits, without fail. He's voiced his distaste to me numerous times, but since I refuse to ban Kinsley or her bike from our home, I clean the floors after she departs to please him.

Returning his attention to the appetizers, Ledger adds the final touches to his spread. Brooklyn, who's always fashionably late, makes her grand entrance, projecting an air of nonchalance and sophistication into the room. My nostrils are filled with the scent of her floral perfume from across the room.

Toby appears somewhat bewildered, a fish out of water in this gathering of friends. It's only our second time meeting Toby, so it's understandable that he'd be uncomfortable.

"So, what is it that you do for work, Toby?" I ask, trying to break the ice.

"I'm a journalist for an online news outlet," he responds. "One week I could be doing a hard-hitting exposé on a political figure, and the next I could be writing a blog post for the personality traits of Zodiac signs. It's something new every day, which I love. I get to interview a lot of really interesting people, too."

Already, Toby's shoulders have relaxed and he's smiling, his passion for his work breaking through the initial awkwardness of our group meeting.

Unbeknownst to him, the true purpose of this get-together lies veiled beneath a thin facade. Toby remains unaware of Sam's involvement with The Laura Group and the existence of the group in general. As per Ledger's instruction, Sam told him that tonight is just a social gathering with friends. Having caught a glimpse of the group chat earlier in the day, I'm curious as to how Ledger will maneuver the discussion of our new job in

Toby's presence. He hasn't told me anything, so I'm just in the dark as the others.

"All right, all right," Ledger says, strutting into the living room from the kitchen. "How is everyone feeling tonight?"

Brooklyn rolls her eyes and scoffs.

"Cut to the chase, Ledge," she says, her words laced with exasperation.

"Tough crowd, okay." Ledger sighs comically. "So, I'm proposing a trip. Let's go to Nova Scotia, guys!"

Ledger veils the specifics of this potential client in Toby's presence. Although the details are shrouded, he's revealed that the case's location is in or around Nova Scotia – a seventeen-hour journey by car. Silence hangs heavy in the air, each of us contemplating the implications of such a trip. Sam is especially lost in thought.

"Come on, guys. It'll be fun, right, Beck?"

"Yeah, I think so."

I stand next to Ledger and try to smile as genuinely as I can but feel like it looks artificial, like the way our mother used to smile. Not that it matters, anyway. The only person I need to convince is Toby.

"And where did this genius idea come from?" asks Kinsley.

Ledger pivots, turning around to face Kinsley on the

opposite side of the living room where she sits with Chester on her lap. The moment Ledger turns to face them, Chester lets out a low growl and I try not to giggle.

"We're in our mid-twenties. We'll be settling down soon with steady jobs and families." Ledger smiles at me and I blush. "This might be one of the last trips we get to take together as friends. Texting each other just isn't the same."

Ledger makes eye contact with me when he says this, so I look down at my phone to see a notification from him to the group chat.

LEDGER: A potential client contacted me about her haunted house in a small Nova Scotian town, where she lives alone. The house has a dark history, apparently. She is willing to fund our travel costs and has offered us her house to stay in if we're willing for a weekend. She also said she'd pay "handsomely" for a Clearing, somewhere in the neighbourhood of $10-15k. It's a slam dunk. What do you guys think?

Holy shit.

Almost fifteen thousand dollars for a Clearing? We'd be

idiots not to take this, even if we do have to travel cross-country. The trip would be financed by the client, anyways, so there really are no excuses.

I stare at Kinsley, an urgent look on my face, but she's already got her head down, reading the chat. Kinsley is typically much more emotive than I am. She wears her emotions on her sleeve, whereas I hide mine behind a brick wall. Only Ledger has ever seen me for who I truly am – all of me. But for once, I can't decipher how Kinsley is feeling.

Brooklyn, who's sitting next to Kinsley, is also looking at her phone after cluing into the group text. Her face is immensely easier to read than my sister's. Brooklyn's eyes are practically bugging out of their sockets, much like mine were when I first saw our potential payment. Her pupils might as well have been replaced with large dollar signs, like in an old cartoon. Knowing Brooklyn, she's probably taking inventory of what designer heels to purchase from the upcoming Fall collection. Meanwhile, Sam, engrossed in conversation with Toby, remains oblivious to the message awaiting him in the group chat.

"I'd really like to go, and it would be nice if you'd come with us," Sam says. "It would be a great opportunity for us all to bond."

Toby lowers his voice to a whisper, and I struggle to hear his response.

"I don't know, Sammy… these are your friends, not mine. I don't want to impede. I don't think I'd be welcome."

Ledger abruptly interrupts their conversation when he plops down on the couch next to Toby and playfully drapes an arm around him.

"We love Sam, so we love you, Toby. We want you to come! I found a place that offers a full haunted house experience. And apparently, it's the real deal, not some cheesy tourist trap. The place is steeped in history, and it recently opened its doors to the public as a B&B that doubles as an authentic ghost experience. We actually become ghost hunters and see the haunting first-hand, how cool is that? The owner is onsite the whole time as our host and guide."

Toby looks warily at Sam across the couch, his body turning rigid at Ledger's display of affection, but Ledger doesn't seem to notice.

"I don't know, guys. I'm not really into ghosts, and you couldn't make me watch a horror movie if you tried. And believe me, Sam has tried." Toby shares a thoughtful smile with Sam. "And I'd have to book off work, and it's on such short notice…"

"You work at an office job with computers or something, right? Can't you just work remotely?" Brooklyn asks.

"And if you don't want to be a part of the ghost experience, you can always hang out at the house or go on a walk.

Nova Scotia is beautiful this time of year," I add.

Toby concedes with a look of defeat, which quickly fades into a smile, lighting up the room.

"All right then, but only if it's *really* okay with everyone that I tag along."

Everyone in the room nods their heads in approval of Toby joining us on our trip. But also, in a silent agreement to accept this once-in-a-lifetime job. Everyone but Kinsley, that is. Her gaze is fixed downwards, looking at her black ballet flats, avoiding eye contact and stroking Chester.

Ten

Kinsley

2019

"Why the hell not?"

Sam and Toby just left, and I should really be on my way too since I work another graveyard shift tonight. But I won't be going anywhere until I give Ledger and everyone else an answer, which I've so far, refused to do. His impromptu interrogation is really getting on my nerves.

"I didn't say no. I just didn't say yes, either," I explain, my voice laced with a touch of exasperation.

"I'm sorry, but that's simply not an acceptable answer right now, especially considering the stakes involved in this job and the substantial amount of money on the line," Ledger responds, urgently. "We've never had a job this big before, and I'm not about to let the opportunity slip through my fingers."

I, I, I.

It's always about Ledger.

"It's not my problem if you don't have the patience to wait for me to think it over. I'm not even a permanent member of the group. I only came back for a few jobs to help Beck, and that's exactly what I've done. I don't have an obligation to The Larua Group."

"But you do have an obligation to your sister. If Beck needs you, it's your job as her sister to fulfill those needs to the best of your abilities, isn't it, Beck?" Ledger skilfully redirects the conversation, attempting to appeal to Beck's familial side.

I give Ledger the stink-eye and turn my attention back to Chester, who is still sitting contently on my lap. His short brown and black fur leaves a trace of itself on my leggings, but right now, I welcome the distraction.

"Right," Beck answers. "Like Kinsley said, though, she already came back to fill our empty spot because I asked her to.

She hated doing these jobs because of the way it made her feel, but she was willing to help us out because it helped me out. I don't want to ask her to do anything else. She's done enough."

Beck sits next to me on the couch and gives my hand a reassuring squeeze. I'm pleasantly surprised by her show of support, choosing to stand up for me rather than siding with her boyfriend.

"Thanks," I whisper, squeezing her hand back.

"Fine, don't do it for your sister, then." Ledger quizzically throws his hands up in the air, letting them fall to his thighs with a *slap*. "Do it for the mountains of cold, hard cash we'll be swimming in once this job is done."

He is relentless.

"I'm not giving you an answer, Ledger."

With Chester cradled in my arms, I make my way to the front hall. I retrieve my pink cruiser and prepare to leave. Placing Chester gently into his basket, I press my lips against his wrinkled forehead before wheeling my bike toward the door.

"You can even bring your dog. She'd be a delightful addition to the trip, don't you think?" Ledger asks.

This guy is chock-full of ideas. It's no surprise that he majored in business administration, only to end up a chef scamming people as a side hustle.

"*He.*"

"What?"

"*His* name is Chester," I correct.

"Well, how am I supposed to know that when you dress him in those frilly, girly outfits all the time?" Ledger laughs, oblivious to the deeper meaning behind Chester's presence in my life.

I ignore him and walk out, not bothering to even say goodbye to Beck. The moment I close the door behind me, I hear the muffled sounds of Beck and Ledger bickering, probably about what will happen if I refuse to come. Despite running the business itself, Ledger is awful with numbers and can't balance the books if his life depended on it. And despite my less-than-stellar history with reading, I'm a math whizz. Even if the client is paying for travel expenses, they need me to organize costs and allocate money.

Over the years, and with the help of my favourite teacher, I've developed my own strategies to navigate the world of math in a way that works for me. Visualizing patterns, relying on logic, and utilizing mnemonic devices have become my allies in doing anything from simple mental math to complex calculations. It's ironic that a condition known for its impact on language and literature has allowed me to succeed in the language of numbers. The precision and logic of math offer me a kind of solace that words can't provide.

After the short bike-ride home, I grab a glass of water and start getting ready for work.

I pin back my short side bangs, applying a touch of makeup before stepping into my black and brown uniform. I grab a treat for Chester, offering him a small reward for being a good boy, and switch on the television to provide him with some stimulation while I'm gone throughout the night. Just before stepping out the door, I grant Ledger's wish with a text, giving him the answer that he so desperately wants to hear.

But the truth remains; my mind had been made up the entire time.

ME: I'm in

Eleven

Beck & Kinsley

2006

The day had begun like every other morning in the Rollins household, its routine nature masking the impending tragedy that would unfold later that night.

At 3:35 pm, Beck and Kinsley, having just arrived home from a day at school, entered their home and went about their afterschool rituals. Kinsley carelessly tossed her backpack on the floor in the mudroom while Beck took hers upstairs to their bedroom. While retrieving her nightly homework from her bag, a scream pierced Beck's ears. The scream was so loud, so surreal, that Beck thought it was a soundbite from a horror film. Time stood still as Beck, purple binder clutched in her hand, froze in a paralyzing mixture of shock and fear. The silence that followed was equally as deafening but short-lived, as another wail travelled through the house, shattering Beck's heart.

Beck abandoned her stationery and raced downstairs, her heart pounding out of her chest. Turning the corner, a scene of terror awaited her. Kinsley was crumpled on the floor, while Randy loomed over her with a phony face of concern.

"Rebecca, good thing you're here," Randy said, shaking his head in apparent disbelief. "Kinsley here had a little accident; you know how clumsy she can be. Go grab an icepack from the freezer, would you?"

Beck disregarded Randy and instead, approached her sister, the gravity of the situation etched upon her face. Beck was not stupid; she knew what had just transpired.

As she knelt beside Kinsley, Beck's eyes fell upon a small gash on her little sister's forehead, a visible mark of the fall – or rather, the push – that had brought her to the ground in the first place. A cascade of tears-stained Kinsley's face, her cheeks flushed and red like a siren's warning. In the midst of her sobs, Kinsley cried out for their mother.

"Jesus Christ, stop being such a crybaby! What are you, like, twelve years old now? Grow the hell up."

Fury and protectiveness welled up inside Beck, further fueled by the scent of alcohol that burned her nostrils. The tension between them thickened, and a bitter mix of resentment and defiance hung in the air. Beck consoled her sister and lifted her gently from the floor, her voice barely audible as she corrected Randy's comment about Kinsley's age.

"She's nearly ten," Beck had said. "You'd know that if you got your head out of the liquor cabinet."

Beck regretted her words the moment they left her mouth.

Randy stepped towards his girls, who cowered in each other's arms.

"I'm sorry, I don't think I heard you correctly. You wanna repeat that?"

Beck looked up at Randy, the sorry excuse of a man who married her mother, and then she looked down at her sister, a broken doll who clung to her side.

"You heard what I said." Beck straightened her spine and lifted her chin. Her voice trembled but was brimmed with defiance.

Randy, momentarily taken aback by Beck's act of defiance, attempted to regain control of the situation.

"You're grounded," he barked. "Go up to your room and don't come out until I say so." The altercation should have ended then, at that moment, as it had before, time and time again. But Beck, fresh into her teenage years, had come too far to yield now; she refused to back down. The adrenaline coursing through her veins fueled her courage, inviting her to defy Randy's authority. The fear that had gripped her moments before had transformed into a surge of power that drove her to push back further.

"Great, that's a new one. You do realize that we enjoy it when you ground us, right? Because even if you banish us to our room for days on end, without food or TV, we'd gladly put up with it just to be away from *you*."

Randy's face contorted with anger, a storm brewing within him. For a moment, Beck wondered if she had gone too far.

"Oh, well then, right back at ya. Grounding you brats is like a vacation for me. Makes me wonder what it would be like if the vacation never ended."

His retort cut through the air.

One moment, Randy stood three feet in front of the girls, and the next, Randy was pushing Beck, his rage having finally erupted. The force of his aggression sent her crashing against the wall, snatching the breath from her lungs. Beck's lower lip quivered, her eyes stinging with unshed tears. She squeezed her eyes shut, resolute that Randy would not see her cry. Not anymore.

Without a moment's notice, Beck fell to the floor and Kinsley scrambled towards her. Randy had departed the room, but the lingering scent of alcohol and cigarettes remained.

Beck slowly opened her eyes and when she did, the dam broke. Tears streamed down her face, marking the path of her silent suffering until, twenty agonizing minutes later, Beck and Kinsley's mother returned home.

Twelve

Beck

2019

TWO WEEKS LATER

The sound of gravel crunching underneath the car tires wakes me from my nap.

Chester startles and jumps off Kinsley's lap, scared by the bumpy road. I groan, rubbing the sleep from my eyes. It's a wonder I got any sleep at all since Sam, Toby, and Brooklyn were singing karaoke most of the ride. But where Toby has musicality and vocal intonation, Sam and Brooklyn are tone-deaf.

Ledger turns the wheel, and I look out the window just in time to see a panoramic view of our destination: Mull House. The white Victorian is a Goliath, and easily the largest house I've ever seen. Its faded green roof towers higher than the trees scattered around the property, and a light smoke flows out of the chimney, disappearing into the sky.

As Ledger drives our rental van up the winding gravel driveway, everyone else gawks at the house, too. But the closer we get to the top of the hill, the shabbier the house becomes, its grandeur seemingly dissolving before our eyes. Paint peels off the siding of the house and shingles hang on by a thread. The exterior moulding around some of the front-facing windows is chipped, and the lawn is overgrown and sunburned. Distance provides the house with curb appeal, but a closer examination reveals a house lost to time. Despite its worn appearance, there's a sort of melancholic beauty to the structure. The windows, at least, seem to have withstood the passage of time with grace.

"All right, gang. We're here!" Ledger exclaims, clapping his hands. How he can be so chipper after splitting the 17-hour drive with Sam is beyond me.

Before I can even gather my thoughts, Kinsley leaps out

of the van, her eagerness propelling her towards the trunk to retrieve her luggage, leaving the rest of us in her dust.

Brooklyn, who's also perplexed by Kinsley's sudden burst of energy, asks, "What's her deal?" to no one in particular. Ledger and I only shrug in response.

We follow suit, stepping out of the vehicle onto the gravel beneath our feet.

The moment my foot hits the gravel, I'm overwhelmed by the fresh saltwater air filling my lungs. I never knew the city air I breathed was so polluted until now. Ledger swings an arm around my shoulder and takes a deep breath.

"Ah, that salty sea breeze. See those trees over there, across the street?" I look to where he's pointing and nod my head. "You can see the ocean through the tree branches if you look hard enough. We're so close to the water."

"Yeah, it's beautiful. I've never been anywhere like this before."

Seeing the awe-struck expression on my face, Ledger smiles at me.

"Do you like it here?"

"Well, we only just got here, but yeah. The environment is stunning. It's so different from where I grew up." After a moment, I add, "And I guess where we live now, too."

Memories of my family's humble upbringing in a

rundown area outside of Toronto flood my mind. It was the best our mother could afford as a single parent, and even when Randy entered the picture and we moved into his bungalow, we never had the means to leave the city environment. All our money went to Randy's vices – cigarettes, booze, and scratch tickets.

"Hm, good to know. Maybe we could get a place here in the future." Ledger gives me a quick kiss and walks around the van to get his suitcase. I giddily do the same.

As I'm struggling to help Brooklyn pull out her ridiculously heavy suitcase – seriously, how the hell did she pack so many clothes? – a heavy door slams shut, drawing our attention towards the house. It's the front door to Mull House, and the owner, a beautiful blonde woman in her thirties or forties, is making her way down the steps of the slightly dilapidated front porch. She locates Ledger immediately and introduces herself with a handshake.

Hand in hand, Sam wisely leads Toby across the road to go on a walk, as per Ledger's suggestion. We still need to be officially briefed, in person, about the paranormal activity here at Mull House, and we can't do that with Toby in the vicinity. After the initial meeting, Ledger will tell our client about Toby and the slight complication of his presence, and as long as she can play into our story, we'll be golden.

"You must be Ledger. My name is Jessica Mull, and my

family has called this house a home for generations. It's a bit cliché, I know," she says with a laugh. "I'm really hoping you can help me out. I grew up here, as did my mother and her mother before her. After I moved out, I resided in Halifax. But with my mother's recent passing and no other family members to turn to, the deed to Mull House fell into my hands. I couldn't bear the thought of selling it, so I returned a few months ago and decided to move in permanently. But the paranormal activity has become unbearable. I don't recall it ever being so intense when I was a child, but perhaps I blocked those memories. Trauma has a funny way of resurfacing."

Don't I know it.

"I'm so sorry for your loss, Jessica. Can we come inside and talk some more about what's been going on?"

Jessica nods, leading us up the steps and into the mouth of Mull House. My gaze wanders, taking in the new surroundings, when I notice the perfect blowout of Jessica's blonde hair and her stylish red heel boots. It strikes me as odd attire for such a rural location, but then again, Brooklyn is dressed impractically for the setting, too – perhaps even more so than Jessica.

Walking in front of me, I take in Brooklyn's sleek and sophisticated outfit, one that showcases her taste for high-end fashion. She wears a tailored black pantsuit crafted from finely textured fabric. Her jacket is fitted, accentuating her willowy silhouette, while her pants drape effortlessly down to her ankles. A silk white blouse with ruffles at the collar and cuffs completes the look, adding a touch of femininity to the powerful outfit. Those words describe Brooklyn in a nutshell: feminine and powerful.

Led by Jessica, Ledger, Brooklyn, myself, and Kinsley travel up the porch steps, but my foot nearly sinks through the rotted wood, and I wobble backwards. Still carrying Chester in one arm, Kinsley's quick reflexes catch me from behind, and she gives my shoulder a comforting squeeze, as if saying *I got you.*

Stepping over the threshold of the large arch marking Mull House's entryway, tension fills the air. I consider saying something about the house, making a comment or asking a question, but decide to let Ledger deal with tension, instead. He's always been the best at maneuvering awkward situations.

"You can leave your suitcases and luggage here in the front hall, and I'll show you to your rooms shortly."

We enter the foyer, where the worn marble floors seemed to exhale a silent sigh of faded grandeur. Underneath the weight of countless footsteps, the floor was chipped and cracked. There's an odd sense of nostalgia and melancholy that is almost tangible as if the very essence of the house yearned for the days when it stood vibrant and full of life. A large rug covers much of the worn marble floor, but the carpet itself isn't in much better shape. The intricately designed rug is threadbare and jaded, its pattern and colours dulled underneath the feet of countless footsteps, including ours. The fibres of the rug seem to cling to life, eager to share their secrets and whispers with anyone who would listen.

Above, a tarnished chandelier hangs from the ceiling. Despite there being no breeze or open windows, it sways gently like it's being caressed by unseen hands. The hanging crystals are cloudy, veiled in a patina of neglect, many of them missing altogether.

Jessica gestures to a spot on the marble floor, next to a grandfather clock. I lay my luggage on the ground and check the clock, curious as to what time it is. But the clock is broken; it doesn't tick or tock. It's trapped in time, just like this house.

And to think, this is the only room we've seen so far.

From what I can see from my vantage point, the main floor's interior is as dated as the foyer. Dim wall-mounted lamps reveal chipped, floral wallpaper throughout most of the foyer and parlour area. A monotonously dark colour palette envelopes the whole house. Framed sepia photographs of who I assume are Jessica's family hang on the walls in mismatched casings. Even though the dust has settled on the crevasses of the picture frames, the people within them still look so happy, so united. My family has always been fractured, and so have I. The framed wall calendar in the sitting room, perpetually in the month of November 1991, reminds me of that all too well.

One time, when I was eleven or twelve years old, I asked my mother, "Why aren't we like everyone else?"

"What do you mean, sweetie?" she'd said.

"We had a talent show today but no one came to see me."

"You were in the talent show? Why didn't you tell me, Beck?"

I walked over to the refrigerator and pulled off the calendar, pointing to where I'd written BECK TALENT SHOW in stubby letters on that day's date.

"I did tell you and I told Randy, but no one came to see me. Sarah Smithers had her whole family come to see her play the recorder and she was awful, but they went and saw her anyway. They took up a whole row of chairs and made a lot of noise when she finished her act."

My mother didn't know what to say.

"I'm so, so sorry, my sweet girl. I've been so busy with work and with taking care of your sister that I haven't been all there."

"It's okay, Mom. But you didn't answer my question."

"What, why aren't we like everyone?" I nodded. "How

do you mean?"

"Everyone in my class has parents that love them. I only have you that loves me and sometimes you forget to. Randy doesn't love me. Randy is mean to me."

"Randy loves you in his own way, sweetie." Tears began to well in her eyes but at the time, I didn't understand why.

"Okay, if you say so. I love you, Mom."

"I love you so much, baby girl. I promise I'll come to whatever it is you do next at school. Just let me know the time and place, and I'll be there."

Not even a month later, there was a grade-wide spelling contest, and I was my class's champion competing on their behalf. I told my mother a week in advance and wrote it on the calendar, this time in bold, red letters; I even underlined it twice. She told me she would come but never did.

Seeing Jessica Mull's farmhouse calendar in an old-school wood frame reminds me of my mother and my feeble attempts at gaining her attention. Soon after, I stopped writing messages and reminders on the family calendar and instead accepted the fact that if she wanted to come, she would. Although she never did come to any of my school or extracurricular functions, blaming work, I made it a point to go to all of Kinsley's.

"Are you okay?" Ledger asks. "You look sad, brighten

up."

"Yeah, I'm all right. Just a little tired from the drive."

"At least you got to sleep the whole way. I'm the one who drove it," Ledger says. I scowl inwardly at his passive-aggressive comment. I hate when Ledger tries to look impressive in front of others, even if it's at my own expense. I offered to take turns driving on the trip out to Nova Scotia, but Ledger declined, and now he's trying to show off. He only let Sam take over for him a few times in Quebec and New Brunswick.

The front door opens and closes with a *thud*, the sound echoing through the house and startling myself and Kinsley. Sam and Toby enter Mull House, and Jessica rushes over to shake their hands. I look at Ledger, silently asking if he briefed the owner on the Toby situation, and he nods his head coolly.

Jessica leads Sam and Toby into the sitting room, and we all find our seats.

"All right, it looks like we're all settled, yes? Welcome to my ancestral home, the historic site of Mull House. I'd like to thank you all for choosing Mull House as your destination and making the long journey to the East Coast. I hope you enjoy your stay here at Mull House, and I will be on the premises the entire time to help meet any and all of your needs. Soon, there will be a formal tour if any of you are interested, and tomorrow night, we will embark on our trademark ghost experience!"

Jessica's words hold such conviction that, for a moment, I almost find myself believing we're here for a thrilling experience at a historic B&B rather than our intended purpose for The Larua Group. Toby seems particularly enthralled by Jessica's introduction, his eyes filled with anticipation. From what Sam's told us, Toby is quite gullible, but in a cute, innocent way, he insists.

Leading us from the sitting room into the adjoining parlour, Jessica guides us with the grace of a true hostess, revealing a table set with two pitchers of iced tea and an assortment of biscuits and scones. The room is dark, and despite the bay window that should flood the room with natural light, the ethereal glow seems only to deepen the shadows.

"Please, help yourself to some of the treats and refreshments. If there are any nut allergies or gluten intolerances, please do let me know."

Kinsley picks away at a shortbread cookie, giving a piece to Chester, who's laying comfortably on her lap. I still cannot believe she brought her dog with her on this trip.

Toby pours himself and Sam two glasses of iced tea. While he does so, Ledger nods knowingly at Sam, having made some kind of pre-emptive arrangement to get Toby out of the house.

"Toby, will you help me grab some things from the car?

I forgot my backpack and want to make sure no one else left anything in there, too."

"Of course, sure thing."

The two exit the house and head out to the car, temporarily allowing us to discuss business with Jessica.

Jessica rushes to retrieve her laptop from a nearby side table and sets it on the coffee table before us.

"I have a video that I captured on my cell phone that I would like to show you. They show just a glimpse of the extensive activity here at Mull House but capturing it all on film has proven to be quite the challenge."

With a press of a button, the video springs to life, revealing the very room we now occupy – the parlour – engulfed in an eerie haze.

In the video, Jessica narrates: "It's June 10th, 2019, and I just had a guest over. As I was cleaning up the dishes in the parlour, I witnessed one of the teacups fly off the coffee table. So, I am recording it in an attempt to capture more activity." The camera pans to the shattered teacup on the hardwood, across the room. Jessica zooms in on the porcelain shards and droplets of tea. A creaking, followed by a pitter-patter sound, something like footsteps, is heard. The camera hastily moves across the room to where the door to the basement, previously closed from a shot earlier in the video, is now open. Jessica gasps, and the video ends.

Jessica's voice carries a tinge of disappointment as she explains, "I know it may not seem like much, but it's the only footage I've managed to capture. You understand how challenging it is to obtain concrete evidence of paranormal activity."

"It certainly can be a challenge," Ledger agrees.

"If you'd like, I can recall some of the more terrifying events I've experienced. For instance, I've woken up countless times in the dead of night to find a figure standing over my bed. Its silhouette resembles that of a human, but it doesn't…feel human. It's just a faceless shadow that fills me with terror. I'll also wake up because of this repugnant stench that fills the room, it smells of rotten eggs and feces. And when I open my eyes, there it is, right above me, staring at me. This figure, it's haunted me to such an extent that every morning after I see it, I attempt to depict it through drawings. I took art classes during my youth and found it helps me work through the emotional turmoil I experience on a nightly basis."

Jessica takes out her cellphone and opens her Photos app, and then turns the screen toward us. On the screen, there's a picture of a ghost drawn on a sketchbook page. Despite our line of work, I don't believe in the supernatural – but if I'm being honest, I'm unsettled by the drawing. While it's only a picture of a pencil sketch, the image is just as Jessica described it.

The figure has the unmistakable shape of a human, outlined in black graphite pencil, but the absence of a face leaves an uncanny void in its place. The darkness of its form is impenetrable, devoid of any discernible features that would give it an identity. It looms over a bed, Jessica's bed, and the skilful shading of the shadows create a dark aura around a sleeping Jessica.

"That's just a quick mock-up of what it looks like, but I can't do it justice. It looks worse. And the feeling of dread that comes over me has convinced me that it's something other than a ghost. It's darker than that."

"Do you believe this entity to be demonic, Jessica?"

"Oh, my…" Jessica puts her head in her hands. "I'd never thought about it in those terms, but maybe. Yes. I do. There's just too much activity in this house for me to believe otherwise. Harmful activity, I mean. I've been scratched and bruised and feel nauseous in certain rooms in the house. It feels like pure evil."

"Perhaps we could go on that tour," I suggest. "As our acting clairvoyant, I know I'd like to get a feel for the house and see if I can pick up on any entities or traumatic events."

My act has begun.

The front door opens and shuts once more, signalling

Sam and Toby's re-entry. Sam carries a backpack and Toby has brought snacks with him.

"You boys are just in time," Jessica proclaims. "We're just about to embark on our official tour of Mull House. Would you like to join us?"

"Of course, that sounds great," Toby says.

Jessica leads us into the kitchen with its traditional black and white checkered flooring and through the neighbouring dining room. She tells us various facts about Mull House's history, but I can't be sure whether they're true or fabricated to support the historic B&B narrative. She leads us up the narrow and steep stairway with minimal light to aid in our journey to the second floor.

"All of the bedrooms and most washrooms are located on the second floor. There are a few rooms that are out of commission, though, and are not available for residency. Namely, the playroom and study. There are five bedrooms, four of them with a queen-size bed, and the remaining room has two double beds. Hopefully, this will more than suffice for your stay here."

"That should be great, thank you," Ledger says.

I look around the upstairs hallway and focus on everything I can, straining my eyes to catch the most minute details and spin them into gold. But there is nothing cohesive about this house. All of the doors have different wood stains and doorknobs on them as if the designer couldn't make up their mind. A dirty rug spans the length of the entire hallway, its fabric worn and faded.

"I'd love to show you those inoperative rooms if you're interested. You'll have a chance to explore them yourself tomorrow night during the ghost experience, but we can still take a peek inside."

As Jessica opens the door closest to the stairs, a musty odour fills the air, assaulting my senses.

"This here is the playroom. As a girl, all of my toys were stored here. My mother and her mother were even homeschooled in this room." Jessica gestures to a lonely child's desk in the corner, a film of dust coating the table's surface. "You could say that I'm a collector, of sorts. I never throw anything out, and so everything you see in the playroom has been here for decades."

When we step inside the large playroom, the scent only becomes more pungent. The awful smell is soon replaced by an even worse sight – the gloomy view of innocence lost.

"As an adult, I don't use the room as much as I once did. But every so often, I feel… called to go in." Jessica runs her hand across the dusty roof of an antique dollhouse with chips in the roof. "On several occasions, when I enter the playroom, I hear the sound of children giggling. Toys and knickknacks would be moved around to different places. And one time," Jessica lowers her voice for dramatic effect. "One time, the door closed and locked itself when I tried to leave. I was in here for hours."

The thought of being trapped in a windowless room for hours churns my stomach.

I scour the room, searching for anything of significance amidst the relics of Mull House's past, my fingers brushing lightly against forgotten toys coated in a layer of grime. It's hard to imagine that children once played in this windowless space. While it's possible that in Mull House's prime, the playroom held a different allure, I can't visualize a child happily playing in a space so dark and dreary. When Jessica initially mentioned a playroom, I wasn't expecting *this*. The playroom is darker than any other room we've seen on the tour so far, with not a single window in its four walls. The pale ABCs wallpaper is peeling, dangling like a hangnail waiting to be ripped from a fingertip. I half expect some evil, headless doll to be hiding around the corner somewhere, but I never see one.

With an air of anticipation, Jessica guides us out of the playroom and gestures towards the study room located just across the hall. As we approach, a chill crawls up my spine, sending a shiver through my body. Even after leaving the playroom, the effects of its eeriness remain. Jessica turns the weathered and worn brass doorknob, introducing us to the Mull House study.

Like the rest of the house, the study room is enveloped in darkness, but not to such an extreme extent. Dim light filters through the cracks in the heavy curtains, casting patterns upon the dusty hardwood. The study is a sanctuary of forgotten knowledge, lined with bookshelves that reach from the floor towards the ceiling, their spines cracked and discoloured. The scent of old paper mingles with the faint aroma of something far more sinister, teasing the senses with an intangible malevolence.

No – I'm being ridiculous. I'm letting the eeriness of the house affect my state of mind. There are no ghosts here, and once we do our jobs, we can go home with the largest payout The Larua Group has ever received.

A portrait of a stern-faced man hangs on the wall, his eyes following our every move, guarding the room's secrets. I wait for Jessica to provide us with some historical context as to who this man was, but she says nothing. Jessica gives us no further stories to accompany the study.

"If it's all right with you folks, I'll show you to your bedrooms, now."

Jessica stands at the study's entrance and waits for each of us to pass through before closing the door swiftly.

One by one, Jessica introduces us to our respective

rooms.

The guest bedrooms are in better shape than the playroom and study, but they still freak me out. In the first guest room, belonging to Kinsley and Chester, a towering bookcase dominates the space, stretching from the worn floorboards to the ceiling above. But unlike the shelves in the study, this bookcase is empty, devoid of books and treasures. In the second guest room that belongs to Ledger and me, a collection of vintage stuffed animals adorns the bed. Their fur is faded and frayed, casting shadows that distort their once playful expressions. Among them, a teddy bear misses an eye, its threadbare form imbued with an unsettling feeling of abandonment.

"Don't worry, we'll dump those on the floor while we sleep tonight," Ledger whispers, appearing beside me. I'm inclined to agree with him. "Those things are fucking creepy."

Jessica leads us further down the hallway to Sam and Toby's guest room, which is decorated with faded floral wallpaper. A wooden four-poster bed, draped in tattered lace, occupies most of the space. The ornate headboard, intricately designed with carvings of ivy and roses, hints at the grandeur this room once possessed.

Noticing Toby's rigid posture and darting eyes, Sam tries to crack a joke. "It looks like we got MeeMaw Rose's hospice suite," Sam whispers to Toby, laughing. Toby smothers a smile but eventually gives in.

The final guest room, which belongs to Brooklyn, reveals a cracked tri-fold mirror positioned across from one of the two double beds. The jagged lines running through the glass resemble spiderwebs. As Jessica recounts her chilling encounter, sitting before the mirror, the image of shattered glass fills my mind, the shards suspended in mid-air as if time had frozen, waiting for a fateful moment to descend.

"I've had similar experiences here, in these rooms. I rarely go in the guest rooms unless it's to clean up after we have guests, but I've still witnessed some terrifying things. That mirror in the vanity broke while I was sitting there, staring into it. The glass broke as if someone took a sledgehammer to it, and shards flew everywhere. It almost cut me."

Jessica shudders, and Toby looks like he's going to be ill once again.

"Anyhow, I'll leave you all to settle and unpack your bags. Dinner will be served at 5:30 pm sharp in the dining room downstairs."

We smile, thanking Jessica for the tour, and depart into our respective guest bedrooms.

Ledger jumps onto the bed, his large frame shaking some plush occupants off the bed's surface and onto the floor.

"What do you think will be for supper?" Ledger asks. "I'm starving, and all I can think about is what kind of East Coast dish we'll be eating tonight. *God*, I hope it's lobster, or maybe scallops."

"Supper?" I ask quizzically.

"Yeah, I have some extended family in Newfoundland. It's called supper in the Atlantic provinces, not dinner. Come on, Beck, didn't you do any research for this trip? We don't want to offend Jessica."

I shake my head, wondering just how many native East Coasters refer to the main meal of the day as dinner, and if Jessica is one of them.

Thirteen

Kinsley

2019

ONE DAY LATER

After a relatively uneventful night at Mull House, we've planned for today to be a day of exploring.

"*Carlisle's Convenience.* How charming," Ledger says.

We drive about fifteen minutes to a small convenience

store in Mulgrave, the bordering town where Mull House is located. The building is adjacent to the ocean and nestled in the trees. Its parking lot, barely fitting four vehicles, is partially occupied by a worn-out sedan, prompting us to secure one of the remaining free spaces before stepping out to gather snacks for our day's adventure. Toby graciously volunteers to stay in the van, keeping Chester company until our return.

The sound of bells fills the space when we walk through the door, jingling against the handle. My gaze is immediately drawn to a display of impulse buys positioned strategically toward the cash counter. The gum and chocolate bars have clearly been rifled through, but not reorganized for the next impulsive customer.

A young man sits behind the cash register with his feet on the desk, and he quickly composes himself when he sees us enter.

"Welcome to *Carlisle's Convenience*," he says. "Haven't seen you folks around here before. Tourists, I presume? Whereabouts are ya from?"

"You could say that," Sam says.

"We're from Toronto," I say, accidentally talking over him.

We laugh at the timing of our eager responses.

Ledger and Beck silently break from the group,

wandering down the candy aisle, Sam trailing behind them. I head towards the drink section at the other end of the store.

"I'll keep you company," Brooklyn declares, appearing by my side and linking her arm with mine.

Together, we strut past the cashier, my body jolting slightly as Brooklyn abruptly comes to a halt.

"So, you must be Carlisle, then?" Brooklyn inquires, her voice laced with a flirtatious tone, leaning casually against the grimy counter. She snaps her arms back once she sees the less-than-pristine state of the desk.

While I know Brooklyn isn't interested in the cashier, she's not being cruel; it's just Brooklyn being Brooklyn. Despite her playful demeanour, there's a warmth to her character, a genuine kindness that sets her apart. Ledger, on the other hand, possesses a charisma that masks his true intentions, his true self. Beck remains oblivious to his act, blinded by love and loyalty despite all he's done to hurt her. But I see through Ledger's charade, and I can only hope that one day Beck will see it too.

"Nope, that's my old man," the cashier responds, extending his hand for a handshake. Brooklyn and I exchange uncertain glances before reluctantly offering handshakes in return.

"So, who are you?" I ask.

"Oh, I'm Blake. Pretty cool, right?" he responds with

confidence.

"And what's cool, exactly?"

"My name. It's not too often you come across a guy named Blake," he boasts, a smug look settling on his face.

This guy cannot be serious.

"I actually dated a guy named Blake," Brooklyn says.

"And I have a cousin named Blake," I add.

Ignoring me, Blake the cashier looks at Brooklyn and says, "But my name is rare. It's not spelled 'Blake' with an 'a' or 'Blayke' with a 'y'. It's spelled 'Blæc', with an 'a-e'. It's the Old English way." His head nods up and down with unwarranted swagger.

"That's lovely," Brooklyn deadpans, rolling her eyes.

When I look down at his name tag, the name is spelled 'BLAKE' – the regular way. My hand instinctively covers my mouth, trying to stifle the guttural laugh attempting to escape. But Blake notices my amusement and follows my gaze down to his uniform and name tag. A sour expression washes over his face as he realizes we've caught him in a lie. In a swift motion, he rips off the name tag from his shirt and retreats to the back room without saying a word. Brooklyn and I exchange a knowing glance and burst into laughter, momentarily losing ourselves in the sheer absurdity of the situation while Beck and Ledger appear with a basket of snacks.

"What's so funny?" Ledger asks.

"You… had to be… there," Brooklyn says between wheezes.

Sam, having overheard the commotion, comes running through the aisles, concern etched on his face.

"Is someone hurt?" he asks, his voice tinged with worry.

I can easily see how Brooklyn's wheezing could be perceived as cries.

"Relax, Sam." Ledger rubs a breathless Sam's shoulder in circles. "No one's hurt. That's just Brooklyn's witch cackle. She's been afflicted ever since we were kids, and unfortunately for anyone in her vicinity, there's no cure." Ledger winks mischievously at Brooklyn, and she scowls.

A sheepish smile spreads across Sam's face as he takes a step back. I love that Sam's always looking out for everyone.

Beck directs her attention to the now-empty cash desk, asking, "Hey, where'd the guy go?"

Brooklyn and I share a look and giggle again, but we're interrupted by Blake's triumphant return to the desk. He resumes his duties as if nothing had occurred.

"So," says Blake as he begins to scan our items. "Why is it you folks are here, exactly?"

"We're here on a little friends vacation. Staying at the old Mull House," Ledger replies, his lie rolling off his tongue effortlessly.

I hate to admit it, but I'm impressed by his smooth delivery; although I can't imagine why he feels the need to fabricate a story in the first place. Toby is waiting in the car, and everyone else present is part of The Larua Group. Perhaps Ledger simply has a penchant for lying, a trait that doesn't surprise me given his behaviour while dating Beck.

"Huh. I thought no one lived there."

"The ownership recently shifted."

"Huh," Blake repeats.

For the remainder of the transaction, Blake remains silent, focusing solely on the task at hand. Ledger settles the bill, leaving a dollar tip, and we make our way toward the exit. However, before we can leave, Beck is abruptly pulled backward, caught in Blake's grasp.

"Be careful," Blake the cashier says. He grips Beck's arm as she tries to wriggle away.

"Get the hell off of me!" she shouts.

"Don't say I didn't warn you. That house is bad news. Been abandoned for years." My ears perk at his claim.

Ledger, immediately springing into action, interjects.

"What do you think you're doing? Get your hands off her," he says. Ledger pushes Blake away, positioning himself protectively in front of Beck. Ledger towers over Blake, exuding an Alpha presence that I can only describe as cocky.

Blake looks past Ledger to my sister, cowering behind him. "Remember what I said. Something ain't right there," he warns, cryptically.

"Something isn't right in your freaking head," Sam shouts out. I smile because Sam is typically so quiet, so it's nice to see him retort like that.

"Come on, guys, let's go," I suggest, eager to leave.

We exit the store and quickly usher Beck into the van, her visible distress evident in her trembling demeanour. She's practically shaking in her seat.

"Hey, hey. You're all right," I tell her.

"I know. I just…wasn't expecting that. The way he grabbed me, I know it wasn't too forceful, but it still reminded me of Randy."

"Does Ledger know? About the extent of the abuse?"

"Yeah, he knows everything. It's probably why he was so protective."

"Well, yeah, I'd hope so. Another man put his hands on his girlfriend. If he hadn't lunged to protect you, then we would've had a problem," I assert.

I hate to admit it, but Ledger earned a bit of my respect in defending Beck so fiercely. Though he loses it immediately when he completely ignores the situation and Beck's reaction to it once we're in the car.

As the van doors open and the rest of our group piles in, Ledger turns around from the driver's seat, facing Beck and me in the back.

"Alright, where are we off to now?" he asks, a glimmer in his eyes. "We were looking at some websites on things to do in Mulgrave and the surrounding areas. Becky, I'll let you choose. Do you want to go get some ice cream at the ice cream barn, or do you want to go down to the wharf?"

"We should probably do something first before we get a cold treat," Beck replies, her voice gaining strength.

"Let's go to the beach then and look for some sea glass, okay?"

Beck smiles and straightens herself in the car seat. She's built her wall back up already. I hate seeing her so defensive to everyone and everything; even me. For almost as long as I can remember, Beck has been an impenetrable fortress. Ever since our mom went to jail for Randy's death. According to official police reports, Mom had gotten a hold of it after Randy hit Beck in front of her. The bullet went right through his eye and took out his eyeball.

I've told her that she doesn't need to be so guarded or feel so guilty. After all, there's nothing she needs to hide from.

I just wish that she'd let me in.

Fourteen

Beck & Kinsley

2006

"He did *what?*"

Beck and Kinsley's mother was shocked to hear what Randy had done to the girls. She did not want to believe it, but she also knew the girls had no reason to fabricate such a story. Randy was strict and often mean to the girls, but surely, he had never hit them before – or had he? Wrestling with conflicting emotions and thoughts, the three found themselves at the emergency room where Kinsley received stitches for her deep forehead wound. In the sterile room, a concerned doctor inquired as to the cause of Kinsley's injury, and without meaning to, her mother lied.

"Oh, she tripped going up the stairs and caught the edge of the wooden steps," she had said. Kinsley neither disagree with nor corroborated her mother's story. With only one family member per patient allowed in the hospital room, Beck had remained outside in the waiting room, silently picking her fingernails until they were raw nubs.

The car ride home was quiet but also loud. No words were exchanged, though each passing moment of silence amplified each passenger's inner thoughts and feelings.

Kinsley was tired and in pain from the stitches. Beck was fuming, angry at Randy for what he had done and at her mother for lying about it to cover for him. For their mother, a sense of disbelief lingered, refusing to be shaken off. Her mind raced with thoughts, her heart pounding against her chest. There was also anger, simmering just beneath the surface, directed at Randy for the pain he had caused. This revelation about Randy's actions towards her daughters shattered an illusion of safety, one that she ignorantly believed to be the truth. The night had left her acutely aware of the danger her family faced, and every creak of the car seemed to echo a foreboding sense of vulnerability.

As they approached their driveway, Randy's pickup truck loomed before them, reminding them of the man who had caused so much pain before stepping foot in the house. For a moment, Beck and Kinsley's mother considered turning the car around and fleeing, whisking her children away to her mother's house in Thunder Bay. But reality soon intervened, reminding her of the exorbitant cost of the journey and her financial limitations. Women's shelters flickered as an option, but the gravity of her circumstances remained uncertain in her mind. Was her situation truly dire enough to warrant escaping? Doubt clouded her thoughts as she weighed her limited options. Perhaps she could talk to Randy and straighten things out with him; give him an ultimatum and tell him things need to change. Alternatively, she could simply break things off, once and for all.

Only on one occasion had she tried to separate from Randy. Before they could even have the conversation, she had 'fallen' down the stairs. Though it was the threatening whisper that accompanied his actions that etched fear deep into her soul: "Over your dead body will you ever leave me," Randy had whispered in her ear.

Fear for her own safety intertwined with a profound concern for her Beck and Kinsley. Summoning every ounce of courage she could muster, she opened the car door for her daughters and guided them inside their home, her determination to face Randy for what she hoped would be the final encounter growing stronger with every step.

Fifteen

Beck

2019

The beach is nicer than I thought it'd be. It may not boast perfectly manicured shores or soft white sand, but the Mulgrave coastline is beautiful in its own right.

As we make our way towards the shore, the briny scent of the ocean envelopes me, filling my lungs with refreshing salty air. The distant cries of seagulls and crashing of the waves provide sounds fit for the perfect coastal backdrop. Stepping onto the shore, a mixture of pebbles and sand beneath my feet, I feel a silent tug toward the water. It's as if the current itself was coaxing me, inviting me to immerse myself in the water. I remove my checkered shoes and ankle socks, and cautiously dip my toes into the cool, lapping tides.

My gaze wanders, taking in the full extent of my surroundings. Waves crash against rocks that protrude out of the water, sending up a fine mist that glistens in the sunlight. In his research of the East Coast, Ledger discovered that it's not uncommon to see fish, crabs, and even whales in Nova Scotian waters; and although I doubt we'll see any marine life here, it adds to the seaside town's natural allure.

I begin to walk along the shoreline, clutching my footwear in my left hand. With each step, I take note of treasures that have washed up on the sand, spit out by the ocean. Five unique shells catch my eye against the backdrop of an endless array of pebbles scattered in the sand. Among the scattered debris, I discover three pieces of weathered driftwood, two severed lobster claws, and the occasional glimmering fragment of sea glass. My pockets grow heavy with the weight of these souvenirs, shards of turquoise sea glass and rocks of various shapes and colours.

Turning my gaze back towards the beach, I decide to walk in the other direction, this time along the beach rather than the shoreline. Humidity clings to my skin, and while the salty breeze cools my face from the heat, it also blows my hair around into a matted mess. I wish I'd brought a hair tie.

"Beck! Come tan with me!"

Brooklyn's voice rings out from a short distance ahead, her arms waving vigorously in the air as if she's doing jumping jacks. Finally reaching her, I notice she's stripped down to a dainty black bikini.

"Isn't it stunning?" she asks me, doing a 360 degree turn.

I nod my head, still in awe of the foreign sights, sounds, and smells surrounding us.

Crouching down, Brooklyn spreads out a towel on the rocky upper shore. It takes her all of one minute to realize that reclining on stones does not make for a comfortable sunbathing experience. Laughter erupts between us, and we decide soon after to locate the others.

Sam and Toby walk hand in hand further down the beach. They make such a nice couple. Even though I don't know Toby too well, he makes Sam happy, and that's all we can ask for. Sam's had such a rough go of it recently, especially when he came out to his unsupportive parents last year. At the time, he'd secretly been dating Toby for nearly a year, and they were so in love that he proposed. Toby's enthusiastic "yes" prompted Sam to introduce his new fiancé to his wealthy, uber-conservative parents. Sam was kicked out of the house and told not to come back until he "straightened up," and although it almost broke his heart, Sam told Ledger that choosing Toby was the easiest decision he'd ever made because Toby loves him unconditionally. Being disowned by his family was a brutal blow, but The Larua Group, our tight-knit circle of friends, became his chosen family. I wouldn't have it any other way, and I think he feels the same. Sam's like a brother to me.

Sam proclaims that he wants to go for a swim, and Brooklyn, already clad in her bikini, joins him. Toby finds a large wood log to sit on and captures some photos. Sam whips off his shirt, discards it on the shore, and runs into the ocean, waves splashing behind him as he hits the water.

"Whoo!" Sam yells. He shivers, shaking like a wet dog. "Come on, Brooklyn! It feels so good."

Sam dives underneath the surface of the ocean and swims around, doing a breaststroke. At least, that's what I think it is. I don't swim, but Ledger and Sam were both on the university swim team back in their college days. Even though he didn't pursue the sport, Sam still loves to swim.

Brooklyn dips her foot into the water and jumps backward with a yelp. She eventually enters the ocean so that she's thigh deep. In typical Brooklyn fashion, she never gets her bikini wet, nor does she fully submerge her head. She's the only girl I know that wears a full face of glam makeup to the beach.

As Sam swims around and Brooklyn stands awkwardly, splashing her hands in the water, I take a seat next to Toby on the log.

"Not a swimmer?" I ask him playfully.

He shakes his head. "Nope, not since I was a kid. There was this time I almost drowned in a pool, and I've never swum since."

"Damn, that's awful. I'm sorry," I offer.

"Don't be, it was my own fault. I was competing with a friend to see who could hold their breath the longest, and I passed out underwater. Needless to say, I won." Toby laughs, and I join along. I like his sense of humour.

After a moment, Toby refocuses his attention to Sam in the distance. His smile and the love radiating from him is contagious. We sit in silence for a few minutes, savouring the moment, before I realize what's missing from this scene.

"I'm going to go find Kinsley," I tell Toby.

I leave the scene and walk forward until I reach Kinsley sitting on a boulder. She's on her phone, and the zoned-out expression on her face tells me she's mindlessly scrolling. Chester sleeps on a beach blanket below her.

"Really?" I quip, a hint of disapproval in my voice. "You're on social media *now*? And *here*, of all places?" I snatch the phone away from her and throw it in the tote bag next to Chester before picking up the bag and holding it hostage.

"Hey!"

Kinsley hops off the rock and lunges for my bag. I swat at her as she tries to tackle me, giggling. It's like we're girls again.

"Nope. You're not getting it back until we're in the car on the way to Mull House. Look around, enjoy the scenery."

Kinsley sighs, reluctantly appreciating our surroundings.

"Fine, it *is* pretty nice here. But what's Ledger doing? Why isn't he with you?"

Her question hangs in the air, and I realize that I have no idea where my boyfriend is. We parked on the side of the street above upon our arrival and trekked through the forest that bordered the road to reach the shore. I've walked up and down this whole beach and haven't seen him; the only thing I can think of is that, for some reason, Ledger chose to stay behind in the car.

"I'm going to go find him."

Kinsley shrugs, her attention now captured by the pebbles skipping beneath her fingertips.

I walk up the path to the road, which seems a lot steeper coming back. I stand still, relishing in the quiet of nature for a moment, where I'm close to civilization but not quite. A squirrel scurries by my feet and climbs up the nearest tree. It stops on the first branch and looks directly at me, clasping a nut in its tiny hands. The sound of Ledger's ringtone echoing through the trees scares the creature, though, causing it to scamper further up into the safety of the tree branches.

"Hey, hi." Ledger's voice carries through the air.

I can't help but wonder who he's talking to on our trip. Taking a cautious step up the path, I hide behind a cluster of towering trees and listen.

"I'm on that work trip I mentioned. Yeah, in Nova Scotia." He speaks with a sense of urgency as if he's pressed for time and wanting to finish the conversation without appearing impolite. "No, she doesn't know. I think it's going to stay that way." A brief pause follows. "So, how are things going with... you know, all of that?" He sighs, scuffing his shoes against the dirt as he absentmindedly kicks some stones. "Well, I didn't exactly plan for this to happen, Natalie. No, I know you didn't either, but still. Life throws curveballs and you just have to deal with them."

A clap of thunder startles me. Looking up, I see that the darkened sky isn't merely a result of the shade provided by the trees; there's a storm coming.

"Look, I have to go. It looks like it's about to rain, and

everyone is still outside at the beach. Yes, she's here too," Ledger hurriedly continues. "I'll send you the money when I get back to the city in a few days." Another thunderous boom fills the air. "Of course, you know I'm going to help. It's my baby, too. I..."

My ears ring and I can't breathe. My heart is beating through my chest but it's also not beating at all.

It's broken, again – he's broken it, again.

I double over and vomit.

"Beck? What's wrong? Are you okay?" Ledger emerges from the clearing, shoving his cell phone into his pocket. "Here, let me help you to the van."

"Don't touch me."

"What's going on? Are you feeling sick?"

I wipe a stray streak of vomit from the corner of my mouth.

"Who – who was that?"

"Who are you talking about?" Ledger laughs, attempting to deflect the situation. "You're not feeling well, Becky. Let's get you back to the house."

"Cut the shit, Ledger," I snap. "Who were you just talking to on the phone?"

"Woah, you were eavesdropping on me? That's not cool, Beck."

"That's seriously what you're worried about? Not the

fact that you knocked someone up and tried to hide it from me?" My voice escalates into a piercing yell, the floodgates bursting open. "It was her, wasn't it? That homewrecker you slept with when you cheated on me. What the actual *fuck*, Ledger!"

He neither confirms nor denies the accusation but he turns his body away from me and looks at the ground. I drop to my knees and sob.

"Beck? Beck, what happened?" Kinsley's voice grows louder as she approaches from behind me, but I don't want to talk. "Oh my God, are you alright?"

I don't respond, but she seems to understand and helps me up, giving me a hand as she walks me to the van. Once I'm inside the vehicle, she closes the door and confronts Ledger. He must tell her the truth because she slaps him across the cheek – hard. It's like watching a bad soap opera with the car window as my television screen. They argue back and forth but I don't bother listening to what they're saying. I just want to go home.

Resting my head against the window, I see that the sky has turned an ominous shade of green. Raindrops began to patter against the glass, and in a desperate dash for shelter, Brooklyn, Sam, and Toby sprint up the path, seeking refuge within the van. Kinsley swiftly climbs inside and slams the door shut, leaving Ledger as the last to enter.

As he starts the car and shifts into gear, the rain

continues to pour relentlessly. The windshield wipers can't keep up, and we all struggle to see the road ahead. Thunder roars intermittently, and Ledger doesn't speak a word the entire ride to Mull House.

There's nothing left for him to say.

Sixteen

Kinsley

2019

"I'm literally going to kill him for what he's done to you. That piece of shit."

Beck's mouth makes an 'O' shape, her expression a mixture of shock and amusement. I've been doing a lot of cussing lately.

"You'd think that *you* were the one whose boyfriend

cheated on her and got his hookup pregnant," Beck says.

She tries to smile but it's more like a wobbly line.

I pace back and forth in my room, and when I catch a glimpse of myself in the mirror, my face is flushed, and rage fills my eyes.

"I've just…I've never been this angry before. Never in my life. Well, maybe when I – never mind. I just hate what he did to you. I hate it."

Beck embraces me, but I sense that the hug is more for my benefit than hers. Over the years, she's always tried to be the strong one for us, believing it was necessary because we didn't have any parents. But today, I've seen a side of Beck that's entirely new to me. Despite her initial reaction to Ledger's infidelity, Beck didn't shed a tear. She was angry and sad and betrayed, but she never cried, still believing she had to stay strong.

But today? She collapsed to the ground, vomited, and cried, all within a matter of seconds. While it pains me to see her suffer so much, I can't help but feel relieved that she's finally allowing herself to express the emotions she's concealed behind her self-constructed fortress all of these years.

"Thanks for staying with me, Kins." Beck gives me a kiss on the cheek. "I think I'm going to take a quick shower before we get started downstairs."

I nod in understanding and exit the room assigned to Beck and Ledger by Jessica. Needless to say, he won't be welcome in that room tonight or any night in the future. Yet, I can't help but remember that I had similar thoughts when he first cheated on Beck; a belief that she wouldn't reconcile with him. But she did, only to be deceived once again.

Sometimes my sister reminds me of our mother in the worst possible ways.

Seventeen

Beck & Kinsley

2006

Kinsley had been put to bed by her mother, tired and sore from the day's events. She fell asleep swiftly.

To an outsider, their mother might have appeared like a genuine caregiver, tucking her child in, and attending to her needs. But now, Beck saw through the facade. Their mother moved in and out of the room like a bandit, hastily covering Kinsley with the blankets and switching off the main light.

Beck kept a watchful eye on her sleeping sister, ensuring

her well-being and checking if she needed anything. She gently brushed aside a strand of Kinsley's red hair, revealing the stitches on her forehead; the sight of such a substantial wound on her young face seemed out of place. The stitches reminded Beck of the ones on her old rag doll. Their mother had stitched it together repeatedly, as they could not afford a new doll. However, even their mother could not prevent the inevitable demise of Rayna the Rag Doll when the stitches unravelled, and the stuffing was lost.

As Beck looked at her sister, a sense of loneliness and hopelessness washed over her like a suffocating blanket. Seeking solace, she joined Kinsley beneath the covers, lying in bed with her.

After an hour had passed – or ten minutes, Beck could not be sure which – the sound of the front door slamming shook the house. Kinsley stirred but remained asleep. Beck continued to stare at the ceiling until her ears perked at the sound of a plate breaking, followed by yelling. The loneliness she had felt evolved into anger; the very same anger Beck had felt earlier that day when Randy hurt Kinsley.

Beck was thirteen years old now, a teenager. Surely, she could stand up for her family. Yet, her mother was in her thirties and seemed incapable of doing just that.

A thumping noise echoed through the house.

"Randy, no!"

Beck plugged her eyes and squeezed her eyes shut. She rolled over in bed, embracing her sister, and did her best to drift off to sleep, hoping to escape her harsh reality for a little while.

***

Beck awoke to more banging, except it was thunder rather than Randy's fists.

The rumbling of the thunder had made Beck aware of her growling stomach. That is when Beck remembered that she had not eaten dinner that night.

Carefully, she slipped out of Kinsley's bed and slowly opened their bedroom door. She considered what snack she could have as she made her way downstairs. However, just before Beck reached the landing, she heard a distinct click.

"Sit down."

Beck knew that Randy was not talking to her, but she scurried up a few steps and sat on the stairs anyway.

Randy's tone was angry, but his voice was quiet, even.

Beck leaned forward and looked between the wooden bars of the stair railing. In the living room, Randy stood with a gun pointed at her mother, and Beck instantly understood that her midnight snack was no longer a concern.

Eighteen

Beck

2019

After Kinsley closes the door behind her, I head towards the washroom that links my guest bedroom to Sam and Toby's.

This washroom is as frozen in time as the rest of Mull House. The floor is covered in octagonal tiles, and the clawfoot tub, toilet, and sink stand atop layers of its grime. I search for a towel, but there aren't any to be found. Curious about the water temperature in such a rural area, I turn the shower knob, but no water emerges. I wait patiently for twenty seconds, then thirty, and eventually forty, but still, the showerhead remains dry – not a drop to be seen.

Wondering if the plumbing functions differently in this older-century home, I try turning the knob in the opposite direction, but to no avail. I strain my neck, searching for any sign of a blockage and find nothing obscuring the pipes.

I give up on showering, and because I'm still feeling dirty from vomiting earlier, I decide instead to splash water on my face at the sink. The sink's vintage counter is littered with bottles from either Sam or Toby's skincare regime, though I'm not sure whose. Probably Toby, if I had to guess, because he's always well-dressed and clean-shaven, with dewy skin and gelled hair. His well-kempt appearance can be attributed to his career as a journalist, having to interview people in a professional capacity, I suppose.

I move a bottle of moisturizer to the side and approach the faucet, but when I turn the handle to the right and then to the left, nothing happens.

I begrudgingly go back to my room, settling on changing into a pair of black leggings and a black blouse. My hair is still tangled from being at the beach, so I grab my comb and stand in front of the mirror. With each stroke of the brush, I find myself staring at my reflection and can't help but feel the weight of brokenness within me.

Nineteen

Kinsley

2019

When I reach the bottom of the stairs, Jessica is waiting to escort me to the dining room.

"Where is your sister, dear?"

"She's just taking a shower."

"Tsk, tsk," she tuts, disappointment etched in her voice.

"The upstairs plumbing doesn't work, unfortunately. I suppose I should have told you all that, my apologies."

"I'll go up and tell her, then."

"She'll figure it out on her own. Come, have some dinner. You all have a busy night ahead of you."

With graceful precision, Jessica pulls out my chair for me at the grand table where everyone else is already seated. My gaze sharpens like daggers aimed at Ledger, who engages in conversation with Sam about his engagement with Toby. The audacity of this man to discuss commitment and relationships only fuels my anger. When Ledger makes a comment about him and Beck being as happy as Sam and Toby, I just about lose my cool. As I teeter on the edge of losing my composure, Jessica re-enters the dining room, pushing a caddy laden with take-out bags. Ledger's expression shifts, a mixture of surprise and disappointment, as he likely anticipated a lavish seafood feast at the mansion, like the one we had last night.

"I actually read ahead on the best places in the area to get food and asked Jessica to get take-out for us. To have the real tourist experience," I say.

"Yes, these are some of the most popular items from the diner adjoined to a gas station just outside of Mulgrave. I practically ordered everything on their menu, from poutine to seafood platters and their famous coconut cream pie," Jessica explains, sparking enthusiasm around the table, particularly in Brooklyn. That girl loves desserts and anything with sugar in its ingredients, though you'd never know it from her fit figure.

Jessica finishes unloading the trolley cart and wheels it back to the kitchen. Creaky noises from the stairs indicate that Beck is finally coming down from her failed attempt to shower. However, to everyone's surprise, she fails to appear. The stairs continue to groan and protest despite the absence of any footsteps. Jessica, hearing the sounds from the kitchens, rushes into the dining room to investigate, but as soon as she approaches, the noises cease abruptly.

"That, my friends. That is what I deal with every day, except sometimes it doesn't stop so easily."

Toby looks like he's going to be sick, and Sam puts his arm around his shoulder in an attempt to comfort him.

Jessica returns to the table. We begin to eat, with almost everyone opting for seafood of some sort. It is the East Coast, after all. Just as I am about to savour my first bite of shrimp, the creaking resumes, sending a collective shiver through the room. Moments later, Beck emerges at the foot of the stairs.

"What are you all staring at? Oh, that smells delicious!"

Beck takes her seat next to me, her posture upright and her head held high. Ledger, unable to resist, attempts to engage her in conversation.

"Beck, can we talk?" Ledger asks.

Much to my delight and surprise, Beck completely ignores him, leaving his words hanging in the air. Sam, always trying to be the peacemaker, interjects, his hands resting on the table as he takes a deep breath, attempting to diffuse the tension saturating the room. Except this time, Sam doesn't know what he's talking about – he doesn't know the awful things Ledger's done to my sister.

"Beck, come on," Ledger says.

"Guys, let's just enjoy this wonderful food Jessica got for us. Thank you, we really appreciate it," Sam pleads, his eyes briefly closing. He despises conflict and can't help but sense the mounting unease. It's a quality I usually admire in him, but it's really annoying right about now.

"Sam's right," Toby says. "Jessica, your service here at Mull House is amazing, even if the house itself is a bit spooky. I'm going to give you five stars on all the travel sites when we get home."

"Thank you, and it's my pleasure, really. You all came such a long way, so the least I can do is feed you," Jessica says with a friendly laugh.

Throughout the dinner, Beck remains silent, refusing to say a single word to Ledger or anyone else. Sam and Toby try to ease the discomfort, engaging in small talk with Jessica, but my attention remains fixated on Beck and Ledger. I watch Ledger's stolen glances and his puppy dog eyes, and whisper to Beck, drawing her attention.

"You see that?" I say to her, my voice hushed.

The next time Ledger looks at Beck, she meets his gaze head-on, her eyes locked with his. A mischievous smile tugs at her lips as she skewers a piece of lobster with her fork, silently conveying a message of her own.

Twenty

Beck

2019

"All of the cameras are in place."

After our awkward dinner, we prepare for nightfall and the "Mull House Horror Experience". Unlike the rest of us, Toby actually believes in ghosts. The Larua Group knows that ghosts aren't real, and we capitalize on those who believe otherwise. Toby's inherent kindness, coupled with his convictions and apprehension of the supernatural, guarantees his strong disapproval of exploiting those who genuinely believe in ghosts. This is precisely why Sam deceives him on all matters concerning The Larua Group.

As such, preparations were made, and precautions taken, to assure that both The Larua Group's con on Jessica and Sam's lie to Toby remain unchallenged.

As part of the *immersive experience* at Mull House, guests are allowed to set up their own ghost-hunting equipment. So, in case Toby asks about the equipment, we've covered our tracks. Fortunately, though, most of our cameras and tripods were compact enough to fit into the numerous bags we packed, and the rest of our handheld devices could be discreetly concealed in our backpacks or purses. Since we managed to smuggle our covert equipment without raising Toby's suspicion, he believes that all this professional gear belongs to Mull House, courtesy of Jessica.

"I guess your tech background is coming in handy," Toby remarks to Sam after helping him with the camera setup.

"Yeah, I guess it's a good thing I'm here. No one else knows how to set any of this stuff up." Sam laughs awkwardly.

"That was so much fun, but mostly because you were doing all of the work for me," Toby laughs. Sam playfully punches him in the arm. "Can you believe we're staying in a real haunted house? I feel like I'm going to have a heart attack every time I turn a corner too quickly."

"I can hardly believe it myself."

Gathering us in the living room, Jessica proceeds with the pre-ghost experience debriefing, making necessary adjustments for our tourist narrative along the way. Kinsley brings Chester, like she often does when she feels nervous or uneasy. Kinsley dislikes lying; and to be honest, I share that sentiment. No one *likes* to lie, but sometimes a good lie is necessary, and you have to tell it over and over again until it becomes the truth. Unbeknownst to my sister, I've been living a colossal lie for so long that it's been ingrained in my identity.

"I'd like to formally welcome you all to the Mull House Horror... Experience!" Jessica's brow furrows momentarily, but she swiftly recovers. "I hope you all enjoyed setting up some of our state-of-the-art equipment; it's what some of our guests call their favourite part of the experience. As the sun sets, you will begin using this equipment to search for some ghostly encounters all throughout the house, and that goes for the playroom and study upstairs, as well. You have exclusive and unprecedented access to this historic site. How does that sound?"

Ledger's face lights up with enthusiasm, and Toby joins in with an applauding gesture. Sam follows suit, clapping his hands.

As Jessica concludes her speech, we wait in anticipation of nightfall. Stepping a few paces away from the group, I approach the bay window and gaze out at the horizon. Peeking through the trees across the road, storm clouds gather, casting shadows over the sky, and rain begins to fall. The sun is slowly swallowed by the vast expanse of the ocean, and then – darkness.

***

It would be an understatement to say that the group was worried about Toby tagging along with us during this job, but Jessica is proving to be quite helpful in the cover-up.

Aside from a few verbal slips that went undetected by Toby, her act as the hostess of Mull House is convincing. Jessica even offered to stay downstairs in the parlour with Toby while the rest of us move upstairs, each of them unsuspecting to the truth. Jessica thinks we're getting rid of the ghosts that plague her home, while Toby thinks we're experiencing a ghost hunt at a tourist trap. And since Jessica volunteered to stay with Toby, our job just became worlds easier. Typically, our clients are breathing down our necks and present during every aspect of The Clearings we perform, which is why my clairvoyant act is so crucial; it brings a layer of legitimacy to what we're doing. None of that is necessary at Mull House, though, making it one of our biggest payouts for the least amount of work.

We begin to ascend the staircase when I hear fervent whispering. I turn around and see Sam and Toby in the hallway, facing each other, in the midst of a heated – albeit hushed – argument.

"Great, now everyone is looking," Sam says.

"I just don't want to be left alone here," Toby whispers. "It's creepy."

"You won't be alone; you'll be with Jessica."

"I just don't get it. You always tell me to do things outside my comfort zone. I come on this trip with you and your friends, and I'm volunteering to participate in this… this ghost *thing* even though I'm terrified. But now you're telling me you don't want me there?" The look on Toby's face breaks my heart, because he's right. He has every right to be upset.

Sam wouldn't come on this trip without bringing Toby, but Toby never wanted to come in the first place. Even though he's bonded with the group, Toby probably feels like an outsider. Of course, he wouldn't want to be left alone.

"I don't know what else to say," Sam replies, no longer whispering. "I just want to share this experience with my friends."

Both Sam and Toby visibly wince; Toby because it

stings, and Sam because he has to lie and hurt his fiancé.

"Why did you even bring me in the first place then?" Toby asks, throwing his hands up.

Kinsley, Ledger, Brooklyn, and I watch from the staircase, not quite sure what to do. Jessica is standing off to the side, awkwardly looking at her feet.

"Because I wanted us all to bond and share a once-in-a-lifetime experience together." Sam peers over Toby's shoulder and subtly glances at us. "You sitting out during one activity isn't going to make or break the trip."

Sam's being harsher than I've ever seen him before. While he has a penchant for sarcasm and sometimes attitude, he's never cruel. But Sam knows that Toby can't join us, and we have to get started soon, so he's doing whatever it takes to keep Toby away.

"We'll be back down in no time," Sam continues. "All right, are you guys ready to go ghost hunting?"

All of us on the stairs nod our heads and mumble, not wanting to get too involved.

Toby sulks down the hall and into the parlour, Jessica following his lead. I feel bad for Toby, but it needed to be done. Once we finish our job, Sam and Toby can make up.

With The Larua Five finally together, we ascend the staircase. The house is significantly darker after sunset, as there is a disproportionate ratio of light fixtures to windows letting in natural lighting. Earlier today, Jessica set up some candles around the house, though, so we should have no problem finding our way around.

Once we're in the upstairs hallway, we go into one of the guest bedrooms to begin our trademark service – a Clearing. I hang back with Kinsley and let Ledger lead the way, not wanting to be any closer to him than I have to be.

Sam and Brooklyn stand behind the camera and tripod, which is angled near the four-post canopy bed.

"I've got to admit, I'm a little unsure about my *clairvoyance* for this job. There wasn't anything concrete in the house that I could use to make deductions. I guess it doesn't matter though if we don't have her watching us," I whisper to Kinsley, referring to Jessica.

"Yeah, it should be okay. Jessica seems like she just wants peace of mind, and hopefully, she won't need any evidence of the ghosts being gone other than our word."

Kinsley moves towards the bed, sitting down on the mattress and tapping her foot on the hardwood.

Sam hits a button on the camera, still frowning from his interaction with Toby downstairs, and gives Ledger a less-than-enthusiastic thumbs-up.

"This is The Larua Group, here at Mull House in

Mulgrave, Nova Scotia in June of 2019. The owner, Jessica Mull, has reported experiencing some ghostly encounters since moving back into her family home, including, but not limited to, apparitions, unexplained noises, and —"

"It's not working," Sam says, interrupting Ledger's flow.

We all find ourselves with a confused look on our faces at this bump in the road. We've never had issues with our equipment during a job before.

"What do you mean 'it's not working'?" Ledger asks.

"I mean, the camera won't turn on."

"Didn't you charge the battery before?" Brooklyn asks.

"Of course, I did. I charged all the equipment, and I tested them to make sure they worked when Toby and I went room-to-room during the set-up." He frowns at the mention of Toby's name.

"Maybe the battery got fried," I suggest. It's the only thing that makes sense.

"Well, whatever happened, let's just grab one of the other cameras so we can get a move on."

"Of course, this happens today with this job." Ledger stomps out of the room like a child who didn't get their way.

If you ask me, he's a child that got his way, and then some.

"God, it's just a camera. We have, like, five of them

here," I mumble.

"Uh, guys?"

We step out into the hall and follow Ledger's voice into the next guest bedroom, where the tripod is knocked over and the EMF detector, previously on the chest of drawers, is on the floor.

Sam rushes to the fallen camera and unscrews it from the tripod's base, before showing the cracked lens to the group.

"How did this even happen?" Sam's eyes well with tears like he's just lost one of his children. The Larua Group technology is like his child, though, so it makes sense he'd be upset about losing two of his cameras and the EMF detector. He invested so much time and effort into them.

Kinsley volunteers to grab another camera, but what should take her twenty seconds takes her two minutes. When she rushes into the guest bedroom, she tells us the worst possible news: "They're all broken. Everything is damaged somehow."

Ledger throws his hands up in the air. Kinsley and Brooklyn both look discouraged. Sam is just plain confused.

As the shattered pieces of our equipment lay strewn across the room, the broken glass, chipped plastic, and cracked screens seemed to mock us. And that's when it hits me.

This job was the last of the money I needed to save for my degree. It was going to pay for my tuition so that I could start school this fall when I would've had to wait another year otherwise. If our equipment is broken, then we can't do our job. At least, not convincingly enough for that large of a payout. And if I'm not with Ledger anymore, then I'll have to live with Kinsley or get my own place and have my own expenses. So, it'll probably take even longer to save up the extra money for university.

The weight of the situation presses down on me like an anchor, threatening to drag me into the depths of despair. First Ledger, now this job; my future is crumbling before my eyes now crumbling before my eyes.

For the second in two days, I fall to my knees and cry.

Twenty-One

Kinsley

2019

Ledger steps forward to pick Beck up off the floor, but I step in front of him, a human shield guarding my sister against him.

"No."

"She needs my help."

"Beck doesn't need anything from you right now or going forward. Get out of the way."

Brooklyn, who's likely clueless about her brother's wrongdoings, joins me in supporting Beck, helping to guide her gently towards the bed where she continues to cry.

"I've never seen Beck like this before," Sam whispers to me. "Is she okay?"

As we all float to the opposite side of the room, Sam and I look at Beck, who's evolved into the fetal position on the bed. Eventually, every gaze in the room is turned towards her, as if searching her tears for answers.

"What do you think?" Brooklyn asks, eyebrows raised. The quietness that follows her rhetorical question speaks volumes, silently questioning whether Beck is indeed okay.

"Let's just go downstairs and explain to Jessica what happened," Ledger says. "Maybe she'll feel bad and compensate us for the damaged equipment, anyway."

It's one of those rare occasions where Ledger's right about something; he needs to talk to Jessica.

Momentarily lost in my determination, I begin to head out of the room with everyone else, but as I glanced back at Beck, huddled in her anguish, I realize that my place is by her side. For once, I need to be the one shielding her from harm.

"You guys go ahead. I'm going to stay with Beck."

Locking eyes with Ledger, a silent battle of wills ensues. His smug, knowing expression grates on my nerves and reminds me of his self-serving nature. But I don't say anything; now is not the time for fighting. Ledger leaves the room and I let out a puff of air.

"You're a tomato," Beck says, wiping some tears away with her arm.

"What?"

"You're as red as a tomato," she explains, repositioning herself in bed. "Don't be so angry at Ledger. That's my job."

Beck is cracking jokes, already in the process of rebuilding herself amidst the turmoil. I can't help but be in awe of her resilience. Even in her own time of crisis, Beck manages to worry about everyone but herself.

"I'm worried about you, Beck," I confess, my voice filled with concern.

"I know. I appreciate that you care so much, but I'll be fine. Really. I'm the older sister. Isn't it my job to take care of you?"

Her reply is lined with a bittersweet mixture of selflessness and self-reflection. She acknowledges my care but reassures me that she'll be fine, always and forever putting my well-being ahead of her own.

"Maybe a decade ago, but not now."

"I'll always look out for you first, you know. I'm the older sister, it's in my DNA." Beck pats my hand. "With everything you've been through, I can't help it."

"You've been through the same things as me, if not more. You were older when Randy died, and you remember more about him and Mom and everything that happened with them. If it's your job to take care of me, then whose is it to watch over you?"

"I guess our mother's, but she wasn't there to do it." Beck closes her eyes and frowns. For a moment, I think she's going to cry again.

"Exactly. But that's not your fault. She was an adult and made a bad decision. *Right?* But depending on how you view it, maybe it was a good one."

"Either way it's not our problem anymore, Kins." Beck smiles. "We're in a better place now, both of us. No more of Randy or his rules."

"Then I shouldn't have to be your problem anymore, either."

"One, you're not my problem. And two, I know… I'll try to back off more and give you some space."

"Beck, I don't want you to back off. I want you to start looking out for yourself, too. Put yourself first for once in your life. God knows you deserve it now, more than ever."

"I love you," she says, embracing me.

"And I love you."

The embrace that follows, bathed in the soft glow of candlelight, holds in it our sisterly connection. But the moment is abruptly interrupted as darkness envelopes us. A creak echoes through the room, causing us to cling to each other and scurry further into the bed. We feel foolish when we see – hardly – that it was only Chester, freshly awaken from his nap, coming to say hello.

As we give him some pets, Beck and I hear another noise, this one much more concerning: an ear-piercing scream so loud, it spreads through each room and travels down every hall in Mull House.

Twenty-Two

Beck

2019

Kinsley and I rush down the stairs, our fear palpable in every step we take, with Chester waddling behind us.

"Kinsley, pick him up. I don't want him running around downstairs when there could be something…wrong."

Doubts creep in, questioning whether my apprehension is warranted or if it's a part of Jessica's Mull House Horror

Experience to further deceive Toby. But the foreboding feeling in my gut, along with the evidence of our broken equipment and the absence of electricity, tell a different story.

As Kinsley and I reach the main floor and round the corner, we see that everyone is standing in a cluster in the parlour. This whole level of Mull House is awash in an eerie stillness, everyone frozen like statues. I give Kinsley a look that tells her to stay back and go into the parlour. As I approach the group, my voice freezes. I want to inquire about the scream and why they're all gathered here, and I'm desperate for answers, but no words leave my throat. The silence hangs heavy in the air, refusing to surrender any information until I'm finally able to utter those two words.

"What happened? Who's scream was that?"

No one replies.

Ledger turns, a disturbing expression on his face, and speaks with a voice that feels foreign and unnerving. "Beck, don't come in here. You too, Kinsley," he warns.

In no context would I ever listen to Ledger after what he's done to me. Defiance takes hold of me as I stride past him, my curiosity overriding any sense of self-preservation.

The room is shrouded in darkness due to the power outage, yet the flickering candlelight reveals a scene that scars my mind. Jessica lies sprawled across the chaise, her body oozing blood from her stomach; a butcher's knife protrudes from her abdomen at nearly a 90-degree angle. It's a gruesome sight that reminds me of that dark day twelve years ago, blood gushing out of a single bullet wound to Randy's skull through his eyeball.

The sight before me and the feelings associated with my memories churn my stomach, making me feel faint. My instinctual response is to turn away, to escape the grizzly scene, but my eyes betray me, shifting towards Toby and Sam.

Sam is clinging to Toby's lifeless body on the floor, leaning against the same armchair Toby sat in yesterday, drinking iced tea. Blood gushes from the multiple stab wounds that mar the entirety of Toby's torso, each one a testament to unimaginable violence. My feet move almost of their own accord, propelling me forward, driven by a morbid fascination that compels me to look closer. That's when I see that Toby's eyes are still open – and that they are also empty. Vacant and absent, Toby's eyes have been brutally removed from their sockets, the eyeballs lying on the floor next to his form. In Sam's blood-soaked embrace, he cradles Toby, their connection a tragic tableau of grief and horror.

"We have to call the police," Kinsley says, her voice strained as she juggles Chester in her arms and reaches for her phone. "Of course, no service. Did we have service here before?"

"Actually, now that you mention it, I don't think so," Brooklyn responds in a shaky voice.

"So, it wasn't taken out with the lights, then?" Kinsley asks.

"Guys, it doesn't matter. Two people fucking died. No, they were murdered." I take a weary breath, but it catches in my throat and never makes it to my lungs. I swallow, willing my thoughts to verbalize themselves. "I would have said that nobody should touch the bodies, but…"

All eyes turn towards Sam, who remains silent, gripped by an immeasurable sorrow I can't even begin to imagine.

"It's fine, it doesn't matter right now. So, if we can't call the cops, we'll just drive there. Or at least, find a place with a cell signal," I suggest, desperation seeping through my voice.

"How far will that be?" Brooklyn asks.

"Let's get in the van and find out."

"Sam," I say, approaching the scene again. I close my eyes and try to black out the dead bodies and blood but fail. When he doesn't speak, I say his name once more.

"*Sam,*" I implore, hoping to break through the haze of grief that surrounds him. "Sammy, I'm so sorry about Toby, but we have to go get help. We can't leave you alone here. It's not safe."

Sam just shakes his head and continues to clutch Toby's

body on the floor, rocking back and forth. Helplessness washes over me, my mind grasping for a solution, but finding none. We're truly out of our depth here.

Without notice, Kinsley approaches from behind and her gaze shifts past me. Her grip on Chester tightens as she witnesses the gruesome scene.

"Don't look. Kinsley, don't look over there. You don't need to see that again. Come on," I beg, placing a comforting hand on her back, and guiding her towards the front door.

Ledger leads the way, while Brooklyn carries a candelabra, providing us with additional light in our brief journey to the foyer. But when Ledger tugs at the doors, they don't budge. Frustration mixes with urgency, as we all realize we are trapped inside. I make a conscious decision to let my personal grievances with Ledger fade away, at least for the time being, as the gravity of our situation takes precedence.

Together, we strain against the doors again, our hands burning from the effort, but they remain sealed.

"You've got to be kidding me," Ledger says. "Great."

"This isn't a joke." Kinsley's voice quivers, her level just barely a whisper.

"Is there a back door we could try?" Brooklyn suggests, seeking an alternative escape route.

"I don't know. I don't think so," I respond, my mind

racing. "Let's just break a window or something." The prospect of property damage pales in comparison to the idea of being trapped in Mull House with Toby and Jessica's bodies any longer.

Ledger wastes no time, hurling objects at the nearest window in an attempt to shatter it. But not even a hairline fracture forms on its surface. Disheartenment seeps into my veins, threatening to consume me.

"No," Kinsley says, her voice trembling. "No, no, no."

Kinsley sinks to the floor, her back against the wall, comforting Chester in her arms, tears welling in her eyes.

"Hey, it's going to be okay. We're all going to be fine," I speak aloud, trying to reassure not only Kinsley but also myself and the others.

Ledger leaves the room and comes back with a chair. He runs towards the window and smashes it against its surface, throwing his entire body into the movement but yielding nothing in return.

"Fuck!" he yells.

"Maybe you can try another window," Brooklyn suggests.

Ledger leaves the room once again, repeating his futile attempts on six more windows on the main floor. When he returns, frustration radiates from his every pore. Taking a deep breath, he closes his eyes, seeking composure.

"Okay." Ledger takes another deep breath and exhales. "Let's split up and try to find an exit."

"That never works out well in cartoons. Or in any scenario, really," I say, skeptical. But now is not the time for sarcasm and skepticism.

"Well, we're not in a cartoon. And we're desperate. What else would you suggest?"

Ledger's retort leaves no room for debate in a situation as dire as ours.

"Kinsley will come with me," I say. "You go with Brooklyn."

"Are we just going to leave Sam here?" Brooklyn asks, dumbfounded, twirling a piece of her blonde hair.

"For now. It'll only make things more difficult if he comes."

"Okay. If one of us finds a potential exit, shout."

Ledger and Brooklyn ascend the narrow staircase while Kinsley, Chester, and I move out of the parlour and through the main hallway. We pass by a few of the nearby windows that defeated Ledger and his efforts.

As we travel further into the mouth of Mull House, raindrops pelt the windows, assaulting their surfaces, and a bolt of lightning strikes in the distance.

Twenty-Three

Beck & Kinsley

2006

The sound of rain *pitter-pattering* on the rooftop was comforting to Beck, but the silence within her house was deafening.

"Randy, please put the gun down."

Beck knew that guns were dangerous weapons, but she'd never seen one before in real life. She also knew that Randy was already dangerous enough on his own; the thought of Randy with a gun in his possession terrified Beck.

"And why would I do that? You betrayed me. Took her to the hospital without telling me. What if they would've asked questions, huh? What if they sent some of those child protector people knocking on our door? What then, huh?"

Randy waved the gun around in front of Beck's mother's face, the metal glinting ominously in the lamplight. It proved impossible for Beck to peel her eyes from the scene in front of her as if she were immersed in a drama film. Only, this was not fiction. This was real life, *her* real life, and Beck's mother was in danger.

"But they didn't! I covered for yo– us. I covered for us. They didn't blink an eye at Kinsley!" Beck's mother blinked her own eyes to hide the tears forming.

"And what if they review her files? What if they come back?" Randy's voice quivered with paranoia and fear, his grip on reality slipping further. This, combined with his bloodshot eyes, revealed his drunken state.

"They won't! It doesn't work that way, honey. It'll be okay."

In a sudden, violent motion, Randy struck Beck's mother across the head with the butt of his gun, causing her to collapse onto the nearby couch. Beck gasped, her heart pounding in her chest, as she watched her unconscious mother lie motionless.

Randy had nonchalantly observed the scene in front of him and shaken his wife's shoulders to test her consciousness, but she did not move; she was knocked out cold. He shrugged dismissively and rearranged her legs on the couch, making himself comfortable. Turning on the television, he propped his feet up on the coffee table, his demeanour unsettlingly casual. He shifted in his seat and removed the gun from his back pocket, placing it on the end table beside the sofa.

As Beck's mind raced, an idea began to form.

Twenty-Four

Kinsley

2019

As Beck and I roam the main floor of Mull House in search of an escape, words fail me, and I'm incapable of speaking after what I just saw – what we *all* just saw.

Trauma affects every person differently; for me, that typically means crying until my tear ducts run dry. But this time is different. I'm shut down, unable to open the floodgates no matter how hard I try.

Beck takes charge, guiding us down the many dark hallways of Mull House, and I willingly follow her lead. Adrenaline courses through me, intensifying with each step that takes us further into the mansion.

"Hey," Beck says, her voice breaking through my thoughts and stopping me in my tracks. "It's going to be all right."

I look down at Chester, cradled in my arms, and bite down on my lip, my mind wrestling with conflicting emotions.

"Yeah," I manage to say, my voice barely a whisper.

Promises – our mom was always full of them, too, assuring us that things would work out. But her promises of safety and happiness were empty and impossible to fulfill. While I know that Beck's promise is a falsity intended to comfort me, I don't appreciate being lied to. Even in a situation such as this, I would rather have the harsh truth than false reassurance.

Together, Beck and I continue, searching every room and hallway for any sign of an exit, but ultimately come up with nothing. The thunder roars so loud that its reverberations shake the foundation of the house. As rain pounds against the windows, the intensity of the downpour increases with each drop, and erratic bolts of lightning illuminate our surroundings. I can't help but feel that another storm is brewing inside.

Twenty-Five

Beck

2019

I take deliberate, deep breaths, trying to maintain a semblance of composure while Kinsley and I speed-walk through the main floor of Mull House.

Every hallway we roam, each room we explore, turns out to be a dead end. A few beads of sweat form on my forehead and I suddenly feel an overwhelming heat throughout my body.

It dawns on me that there's a crucial consideration I've been disregarding – the murderer may still be lurking somewhere in the house.

None of us openly acknowledged this possibility during our gathering on the main floor, but I'm certain it raced through everyone's minds. Everyone except me, that is. After getting over the initial shock of seeing Toby and Jessica's mutilated bodies, my thoughts were consumed with plans and strategies, overlooking the most glaring fact right in front of my eyes. If the doors are locked, there must be a reason behind it.

Is this an elaborate setup?

Is someone specifically targeting us?

Was Jessica, the owner of Mull House, the intended victim, and Toby just an unintended casualty, or is it the other way around? No, that can't be the case, because The Larua Group is new to Nova Scotia. Besides, other than Jessica, the only person we've come into contact with here is that creepy cashier from the convenience store in town, so there's no one here to target us. Unless maybe… someone followed us here from Ontario.

No, that's ridiculous.

Regardless, I have no desire to stick around and uncover the answers.

A loud bang echoes through the house, breaking me out

of my thoughts and jolting me into action.

"Hold on tight to Chester. We're going to run," I tell Kinsley.

Kinsley nods in the dimness, her features obscured, yet I can still envision the expression on her face. I imagine it's the same mixture of fear and sadness she displayed all those years ago when she awoke to the nightmare of our stepfather's death and our mother in handcuffs. To this day, she remains unaware of my actions that night, of how I altered the trajectory of our lives, snatching away our mother. But I refuse to fail her again.

In the daylight, Mull House was beautiful in an eerie way, possessing a sort of haunting allure. But now, the house is cloaked in darkness; with the electricity out and my vision blurred by the motion of running, Mull House is terrifying, not beautiful. The darkness engulfs us with every step, distorting all of my senses despite only my vision being impaired. My mind races faster than my running, thoughts of different sizes and intensities swirling chaotically within my skull.

We jog down another hallway, hastily checking the remaining two rooms, but they yield nothing but dead ends.

"What do we do now?" Kinsley's voice breaks the silence, her tone tinged with uncertainty. It's the first time she's spoken since seeing the bodies.

For the first time in my life, I don't have an answer.

Twenty-Six

Kinsley

2019

I fight back the urge to cry, to feel anything at all, because I know my feelings will consume me if I let them.

My grip on Chester tightens, and I pet him intensely as Beck and I stand in the darkness of the hall, uncertain of our next course of action.

"Should we go upstairs?" Beck suggests, her voice

wavering slightly. She's trying so hard to be strong, to be the one who saves us all.

"What if the killer is up there?" I counter. My voice shakes much more than my sister's and I make no effort to conceal my fear.

"They could be downstairs with us, too. Or they could be long gone. We don't know either way, so we have to keep moving." Beck is losing more confidence by the second. "Let's go."

We turn around, retracing our steps towards the front of the house, the journey to the entryway feeling like an eternity. Suddenly, I hear creaking behind me and halt in my tracks.

"Beck?"

She doesn't answer me, and I remain frozen in place, gripped by fear. I strain my eyes and ears to detect any sign of her presence but come up with nothing. She's not here.

"Beck?" I call out again, this time a little louder, but I restrain myself from screaming her name in case the killer is still lurking nearby. After she doesn't answer me a second time, I decide to remain quiet, with deafening silence as my only response.

I need to find my sister, and I can't do that in a house coated in darkness. Candlelight is not enough, and there are no candles in this hallway.

During our search, both Beck's and my phones had nearly drained their batteries, rendering the flashlight feature a risky option. But, if there was ever a time to use whatever battery life I have left, that time is now. Shifting Chester to one arm, I retrieve my phone from my back pocket with the other. With a tap, I activate the flashlight, a burst of blinding light fills the immediate area, causing my eyes to burn; I quickly avert my gaze. After a moment, my vision readjusts, and I begin to search for Beck.

The first thing I notice is that I'm in the front entryway, closest to the parlour and dining room. I peek my head into the dining room, almost stumbling on a chair despite having the flashlight to aid me. Turning around, I find myself back in the main hallway, with a large clock adorning the wall and framed pictures that line its length. I locate the staircase, and relief washes over me – Beck must have gone upstairs in search of Brooklyn and Ledger, thinking I was behind her.

Climbing the steps, the floorboards creak under my weight. From the corner of my eye, I catch a glimpse of the murder scene. Every instinct I have tells me to look away, but something feels off. With hesitation, I stop halfway up the stairs and return to the main floor to investigate.

Approaching the parlour, I point my phone toward the scene, bracing myself for the sight of dead bodies. At that moment, I hear a gasp, but realize soon after that the noise came from me. My phone's battery finally dies, but not before I catch a glimpse of the room – the empty room.

Sam is gone.

The bodies are missing.

Before I can process the implications of what I just saw, something suddenly covers my head, and I'm violently pulled backward, my sight consumed by darkness.

Twenty-Seven

Beck & Kinsley

2006

Beck remained perched on the staircase, carefully watching the scene unfold below.

For what seemed like an eternity, Beck had contemplated her plan, calculating every step and every consequence. Fifteen minutes, perhaps more, had ticked away in her mind's restless clock before her mother stirred from unconsciousness on the threadbare couch. Like clockwork, Randy's elbow jabbed her side, a crude wake-up accompanied by a slurred greeting.

"Good morning, sunshine."

Beck recognized the all-too-familiar signs of Randy's intoxication. Her mother often employed the term 'drunk' to both label him and justify his actions.

"Oh, he had too much to drink. He was drunk, he didn't mean it," she would say, a flimsy shield for his behaviour. But Beck knew better. Although she did not yet grasp the intricacies of being drunk, Beck understood that it was far from benign.

Beck's mother ceased her movements, slipping back into either sleep or unconsciousness – Beck was not quite sure which. Memories of the countless times Randy had inflicted harm upon her, Kinsley, and their mother flooded her mind. She thought about her mother, who adored her daughters fiercely but remained trapped in a toxic marriage. Beck's heart ached as she envisioned Kinsley, growing older and bearing the brunt of even harsher mistreatment. Beck would turn eighteen and move out of the house years before Kinsley would, leaving her alone to suffer Randy's wrath. A surge of determination coursed through her, causing Beck to clench her fists and wipe the residue of sleep from the inner corners of her eyes.

Beck had made her decision – she would disarm Randy, call the police, and save her family. They would finally be rid of his presence, and her family would be saved.

Twenty-Eight

Beck

2019

I reach the top of the stairs and a surge of panic courses through me as I realize Kinsley isn't with me.

"Kinsley?" I whisper.

The second floor is slightly more illuminated than the ground level, with more candles spread out on side tables throughout the hallway. Despite the subtle improvement, when

I turn around to peer down the steep staircase, darkness obscures my vision, denying me the sight of any presence – human or otherwise. I take a few measured steps in each direction but nearly trip, avoiding a nasty fall down the stairs.

Trembling uncertainty grips my bottom lip, causing it to quiver involuntarily, and I instinctively place a shaking hand over my mouth in an attempt to stop the tremors. I can't do this alone, I just can't. I race through the upper main hall, a whirlwind of fear and determination propelling me forward with every step. My head swivels in every direction, searching for Ledger and Brooklyn so that they can help me find Kinsley. While Kinsley and I were hunting for an exit downstairs, Ledger and Brooklyn didn't make any signal to indicate that their search yielded anything helpful. Their efforts, like mine and Kinsley's, had yielded nothing to help us escape Mull House.

Kinsley.

I cannot believe I lost her. How the hell did I let this happen? The question echoes relentlessly through every corner of my mind, torturing me with its unanswerable taunt.

As I approach the dead end of the dimly lit hallway, I hear the distinctive sound of paw pads and claws on the hardwood floor behind me. The sound freezes me in my tracks, and I hear Chester's low, unmistakable growl. If Chester made it upstairs, then why isn't Kinsley here, too? She would never willingly leave her dog alone.

I waste no time retracing my steps and following the intermittent sound of his growls into yet another hallway; one I hadn't yet explored.

Swallowing the lump of apprehension lodged in my throat, I sink down to his level and try to pet him. He twitches before my hand touches his fur, something he's never done before.

"Hey, it's okay buddy," I say, trying to comfort him.

He sits on the hardwood, his gaze fixed upon a distant point further into the hall, his behaviour betraying a mix of fear and vigilance. My own gaze follows Chester's, and in the dim light, I'm able to discern something sprawled across the floor.

Or rather, someone.

Holding my breath, I let my feet slowly carry me toward the figure as if the impending revelation were weighing me down. Each step holds more dread than the one before it, and as I finally reach my destination, I throw my hands over my mouth to stop the scream threatening to escape.

Brooklyn lies motionless on her back, a puddle of crimson emanating from her head wound and pooling on the floor. The hardwood is also stained under her torso, where I see that there's another wound in the middle of her abdomen. I blink away the tears pooling in my eyes, willing them to dissipate until

I can get Kinsley and me to a safe location. Once again, against all reason, an inexplicable compulsion draws me closer to her body, and it's a decision I swiftly come to regret.

An object is protruding from the wound in Brooklyn's abdomen, and as I inch closer, I realize beyond comprehension that the weapon is a high heel.

When I look at Brooklyn's shoes, I see that one foot is bare; someone callously impaled her with the dull heel of her own stiletto.

Those red pumps were one of Brooklyn's favourite pairs of shoes. She wore them at nearly all of our Larua jobs despite having a large enough wardrobe to ensure that no article of clothing was ever worn twice. My stomach flips at the thought of the elegance of her favourite shoes being transformed into an instrument of horror.

Panic surges through my veins, and I realize that now, more than ever, I need to get Kinsley and me out of this house.

After witnessing the aftermath of Brooklyn's murder, there's a gnawing concern for Ledger and his well-being eating at my consciousness. After everything that's happened between us, all of the things he's done to betray my love and trust, I shouldn't care about him. But the grim reality of three lives now lost outweighs my personal grievances. Kinsley, Sam, Ledger, and me – we're four survivors in this hellish nightmare, and our only course of action is to escape this house and alert the authorities.

My nostrils sting at the subtle hint of acridity tinging the air, the faint aroma of smoke beginning to travel through the hallway. While I figure that one of the candlewicks must have burnt out, all of the candles in my line of sight remain lit. The scent of smoke becomes stronger, and although every fibre of my being is telling me to retreat, to abandon this perilous path, I press on, towards the smell.

I scoop Chester into my arms, his presence providing me with a semblance of calmness in the face of this nightmare.

Guided by the faint whiff of smoke, I abandon Brooklyn's body and navigate the maze-like halls until I find the source. Finally, I reach the playroom, its entrance ominously shut tight. Smoke seeps from the narrow crevice beneath the door and even spills out the keyhole in the door frame. From within, I hear a string of strained coughs and a cry for help.

"Ledger?" I call out, my voice tinged with both fear and hope.

"Beck? Beck, Becky. Oh my God. Can you help me get this door open? I was walking with Brooklyn, trying to find an exit, and somehow, we got separated, and the next thing I know, I'm locked inside this creepy fucking toy room. Half of the room is on fire now, and it keeps spreading. *Please* help me," Ledger pleads, his voice thick with desperation – and smoke.

"Did you see who it was? Do you remember anything else?"

Ledger coughs. The smoke is starting to thicken, and so I take a step back. How the hell did a fire start when the electricity is out? Unless… someone set it deliberately.

"*No!* Now is not the time. Just help me get out, Becky? I'm sorry for everything that's happened between us, but I love you and I know that you love me, too. I know you do. We can still be happy together."

Ledger coughs, the smoke encroaching upon his lungs, forcing him even closer to the door that separates us. As the smoke continues to spill out of the cracks framing the door, I step back from the thickening haze.

"Happy together as you raise a child with someone else?" I retort.

"Beck, please!" Ledger coughs again, the urgency evident in his plea. "Not the time, please."

In that moment, I realize that Ledger's right. It's not the time for sarcasm. It's the time for reflection and for strategic thinking and decision-making.

So, I think.

I think about me and Ledger, retracing the last two years of our lives and the terrain of our relationship. I think about our movie marathons and the lavish meals he'd cook for me. I think about our dreams of a future home and family together.

But woven in with our happy memories are the passive-aggressive comments, the infidelity that strained our connection, and the lies that betrayed my trust. I think about Ledger having sex with some other girl an hour after telling me he loved me. I think about Ledger getting his one-night stand pregnant and lying about it to my face for months. I think about how he made me feel like he loved me despite all of this, and how time after time, he roped me back into staying with him. I think about how I hate that Kinsley was right about the way he treats me. I think about how I've never truly realized how awfully he treated me he was to me for years and years, until this very moment.

I think about my mother's abusive relationship with Randy, and how she was never able to escape that toxic bond until that choice was made for her. I think about the sacrifice she made in taking the fall for me and how she wouldn't want me living this life with Ledger. She would want me to be stronger for both of us, and so I refuse to mirror her path and make the same mistakes.

"I'm sorry." A single tear escapes my left eye, a bittersweet symbol of my decision.

"What? Beck, no. *Please*," Ledger pleads, his cries echoing through the crackling of the nearing flames.

Heat radiates through the wooden door, flames licking at the edges as the inferno rages onward. Stepping back yet again, my eyes are transfixed on the growing blaze. I watch and listen as Ledger's anguished cries crescendo for one minute, then two, and then abruptly fade into silence. Soon after, the door, once a barrier to the fire, succumbs to the flames. Unblinking, I watch as the fire consumes the playroom, along with the man I loved.

Did I just… kill him? I make a conscious effort to compartmentalize this decision and its consequences. I can confront my guilt when, and if, I escape Mull House – and I have to believe that it'll be the former.

With determination etched upon my face, I fumble in the dark in an attempt to locate the stairs, their descent the only beacon of hope in sight. I'll find Kinsley and Sam, and together, we'll emerge from this house of horrors, one way or another.

***

Nothing will ever be as shocking to me as the moment when I round the corner and find the murder scene devoid of its victims' bodies. Even Sam, who refused to leave Toby's body, is gone.

Desperate to maintain a sense of control, I try the front doors once more, knowing before I even pull the handle that the goliaths won't budge. As expected, they remain steadfastly locked, the storm outside raging on.

We're trapped within the confines of Mull House. Time is running out, the approaching fire threatening to consume us in its relentless advance to devour the house whole.

With Chester still in my arms, I begin to jog along the perimeter of the main floor. Suddenly, I get an idea, halting my steps in their tracks. Could there be a basement in Mull House? I try to recall my earlier exploration with Kinsley, but we paid little attention to the details, our focus veiled by darkness and the desire to find an escape.

The Larua Five – now, just Kinsley and I– searched both the first and second floor of Mull House with nothing to show for our efforts. While the idea of entering a basement while fire rages above is far from wise, it's the only remaining option I have. If there is a basement, maybe Kinsley sought refuge there after we were separated, and maybe the killer moved Sam and the bodies to the cellar. Maybe the murderer killed Sam, and he's one of the bodies now, too. Maybe Kinsley met the same fate while I failed to protect her.

No, I'm spiralling. I can't think this way.

I try to banish every thought in my mind to the back recesses of my brain, but it's no help – my thoughts refuse to be silenced. Walking through the main floor once again, I enter the dining room, this time, in search of an entrance to a basement or cellar. When my search yields nothing, I enter the kitchen, where I come across a door camouflaged into the room's floral wallpaper, ajar ever so slightly. Clutching Chester in my arm, I open the door with my free hand, and miraculously, all my thoughts vacate my mind, with only the two strongest emotions remaining: fear and hope.

Twenty-Nine

Beck

2019

The blackness of the basement is different from the rest of Mull House. It's equally as dark, but there's a cold and empty air to the space, something anticipatory about its atmosphere.

Or maybe I'm just projecting.

As I descend the stairs, the wood creaking underneath

each step, the thought of losing Kinsley. When I reach the bottom step, I hold my breath and stare blindly into the dark. There could be a killer standing inches in front of me, waiting to strike, and I wouldn't know it until it was too late. Is that what happened to Jessica and Toby? The fate of Sam, Toby, and Jessica haunts my thoughts, leaving me to wonder if they sensed their impending deaths or if they were mercilessly blindsided.

The musty smell of dampness and decay hangs heavy in the air; a stark difference from the humidity and smoky haze filling the rest of Mull House. With Chester in one arm, I cautiously navigate through the dark with my free hand until something cold and dainty hits my forehead. I reach upward and grasp the string of a lightbulb, its faint jingling echoing through the room. Relief washes over me when the room is illuminated, revealing that there is no murderer waiting to strike. In fact, there's nothing at all – no murderer, no bodies, and no Kinsley.

The room I find myself in is bleak, its four cement walls converging with a cold, unforgiving cement floor.

I'm ambushed by the image of my mother imprisoned within a cell; her presence is easily imagined amidst the barrenness of the basement. I envision her lying on a thin mattress, arms cradling her head, trapped in a green jumpsuit, with the weight of her false imprisonment corroding her life. Tears well up in my eyes at the thought of my mother confined like an animal in a cage, rotting away in a concrete box to bear the consequences of a crime she didn't commit. A suffocating lump forms in my throat, constricting my breath, until I find myself gasping for air, collapsing to the floor. It's the weight of my own actions that condemned my mother to a life behind bars – not Randy. I'm the one responsible for her imprisonment, and if I die here, her sacrifice will have been in vain. Desperation seizes me as I realize the impending doom that awaits not only me, but also Kinsley.

I'm going to die in here.

Kinsley is going to –

No.

I will get Kinsley to safety, no matter the cost. Without Kinsley ever realizing it, I took away our mother, and with her, a chance for her to grow up with a proper maternal figure. I refuse to let Kinsley suffer anymore; I'm going to find her and get her out of this damn place, once and for all.

Sweet Chester, with his affectionate licks and gentle nuzzles, erases the tears from my cheeks as I regain my composure and stand tall, cradling him in my arms. It's then that my gaze shifts, no longer fixated on the confining walls of the concrete room, but rather, on a small opening leading to a hallway on the other side. My heart rate quickens, and I sprint towards the hall, leaving behind the fading glow of the main room.

Each step echoes as I travel through the curved passageway, until finally, I arrive at the end. Entering a relatively spacious room with pink insulation dangling from the ceiling, a small furnace crackles, casting a warm glow in the space. The furnace is accompanied by a cast-iron fire poker and some abandoned cardboard boxes. But, like the main room, this hidden area is void of Kinsley's presence, or Sam and the missing bodies.

The basement continues its haunting silence, mirroring the desolation that permeates the entirety of Mull House. My shoulders sink as darkness and disappointment engulf me.

Suddenly, the familiar sound of a gun being cocked slices through the basement, shattering the silence that once filled the room. Without warning, a swift movement catches my peripheral vision, and as I turn my head, I see an abyss of black steel.

I stare directly into the barrel of the gun before squeezing my eyes shut, bracing for the unknown that awaits.

Thirty

Beck & Kinsley

2006

Beck had closed her eyes and pulled the trigger.

Beck's mind was a haze, memories blending with one another, and this was one of the only things she knew for certain. She knew that her mother had woken up, desperately attempting to flee from Randy. Beck's mother had tried to hobble away from couch and towards the stairs, towards her daughters, when she noticed Beck hidden behind the banister, fear etched across her face. She quickly tried to retreat, but as Randy grabbed hold of Beck's mother's long, auburn hair, yanking her back with brutal force, Randy saw Beck, too.

"This doesn't concern you, Rebecca," Randy had sneered. "Go back upstairs to bed like a good girl."

"Let go of my mom and I'll go back to bed," Beck had mustered the courage to say.

"What did you just say to me?"

Frozen on the stairs, Beck remained still as a statue.

"I'm not going to tell you again, girl. Go the hell to sleep."

Beck's mother had made eye contact with her, silently pleading for Beck to comply. But Beck had reached her breaking point – she was done with complying.

In one swift motion, a surge of determination propelled Beck to her feet. She raced down the stairs and into the kitchen, where the landline awaited her. Beck's trembling hands had barely dialled the first '9' of 9-1-1 when Randy threw her forcefully against the fridge. The phone flew from her grasp, crashing onto the laminate tile, where Randy proceeded to retrieve the device and smash it against the countertop. Shards of plastic littered the floor like scattered raindrops.

A pounding throbbed in Beck's head that intensified with each passing second. When her eyes were open, she saw stars, and when they were closed, a dizzying galaxy spun before her.

It was from this point onward, that the events blurred and blended together in Beck's memory.

Amidst the chaos, Beck could hear shouting but could not quite discern what was being said. Her head pulsed in tandem with the beating of her heart, which was hastening with every *thump thump thump*. Slowly, Beck crawled from the kitchen floor into the living room, a sense of unsteadiness consuming her. As Beck stood up, it felt as if she were on a roller coaster, her head spinning in relentless circles, nausea welling from within her. The sensation was so vivid that she even heard the rhythmic thumps of the coaster's cart hurtling along its tracks. It took a moment for Beck to realize that those thumps were not a rollercoaster; they were the sickening sound of her mother's body colliding with the wall.

In an instant, Beck had found herself no longer on the floor but instead, gripping Randy's handgun from the nearby side table. The amalgamation of metal was awkward and felt alien in her small, shaky hands. Beck's head still throbbed with pain, but determination burned within her. *Tonight, this nightmare will end,* Beck had thought. Since the landline was broken and Beck could not call the police for help, she would have to find another way; she would threaten Randy and scare him away.

Beck's mother, whose eyes were already swollen, gasped as she noticed her daughter pointing the gun at Randy, who had turned around and laughed dismissively in response.

"That's no toy, Rebecca. Go on and put that down."

Beck shook her head vehemently; she was so angry that her body vibrated, and her rage seeped through her skin like hot fluid in a container.

"Put that away, you don't know how to use it. Someone could get hurt."

This time it was Beck who had chuckled, the irony not lost on her.

Randy had taken a wobbly step toward Beck, muttering incoherently. And that is when it happened.

Beck had never intended to *kill* Randy; it was an instinct, an impulsive reaction. He had come too close, too quickly, and Beck pointed the gun at his head, squeezed her eyes shut, and pulled the trigger by accident. The piercing sound of the gunshot reverberated through the room, accompanied by her mother's horrified scream as she rushed to Randy's fallen body. Beck sank to her knees, refusing to open her eyes again until she felt the gun being gently pried from her grasp.

"You didn't mean it; I know you didn't mean it, baby. It's okay, it's okay." Her mother's voice trembled with a mixture of reassurance and uncertainty.

In that moment, Beck could not discern whether her mother's words were meant for her daughter or for Randy.

Thirty-One

Beck

2019

My gaze trails along the barrel of the gun pressed against my forehead, tracing its path to the hands that firmly grip it, and then up the arms that extend from those hands.

It's Jessica Mull.

Silent and breathless, I'm unable to speak; my jaw just hangs open like a broken hinge. I hold Kinsley's dog tightly against my chest because it's all that I can think to do.

"Beck," Jessica says. "I've been searching for you all over. You've been a tricky one to find." Her voice cuts through the air, sending shivers down my spine.

With considerable effort, I finally manage to close my mouth, only to find myself gnawing on my bottom lip instead. The weight of Jessica's presence, coupled with the gun clutched in her hands and pointed at my head, sends a wave of panic crashing over me.

"I thought you were…" I gulp, my eyes darting anxiously from Jessica to the gun she wields.

"Dead? You thought I was dead?"

I nod my head so slightly that it resembles a twitch more than a deliberate gesture.

"That was the entire purpose, my dear," she replies sweetly.

"But why? Does that mean that Toby is alive, too?" I manage to ask, desperation tinged with a flicker of hope in my voice.

"Oh, heavens no. That poor boy met with the wrong end of a butcher's knife." Jessica's voice is devoid of any remorse or regret.

"Why would you do that? Toby was innocent!"

In an instant, the end of the gun smacks forcefully

against my forehead, causing my head to whip violently to the side, a jolt of pain coursing through my skull.

"You're right, he was. And if I'm being honest, I did feel a twinge of guilt because of that. But this," she motions to the gun, "I won't hesitate to pull the trigger or feel guilty about doing it."

As I muster the strength to gather my thoughts and make sense of the situation, a pressing question emerges from my darkest fear.

"Where is my sister?" I say, posing the question as more of a statement.

"The last I saw of Kinsley, she was lying unconscious on the floor of the main-level powder room after I put a hood over her head. She was such a doll, very sweet, but too naïve. She trusted too much from the moment we crossed paths."

"What do you mean by 'the moment we met'? You knew each other before this job?" I press, desperate to uncover the truth.

"You ask too many questions," she responds, bluntly.

"And you make too many cryptic statements," I say, gathering all of my courage. "Now, tell me why the fuck you're doing this."

A gunshot pierces my ears, followed by a ricochet of concrete. Chester yelps and burrows into my side. For a moment, my body goes through a rapid inventory, and I realize with a surge of relief that I haven't been shot. But the wall right beside me bears the mark of a bullet's impact. I press my back against that same wall and slowly slide down to the floor.

That sound, that God-awful sound, echoes in my mind, refusing to fade away.

"I'm the one with the gun here, I have the power!" Jessica's scream pierces through the chaos, almost rivalling the gunshot itself. Gradually, her voice returns to normal as she continues, asking, "How long have you been a part of The Larua Group, Beck?"

"A few years. Essentially since it began." I speak so timidly that I don't recognize my own voice.

"Do you remember all of the cases you've worked on?" she probes further.

"To an extent, yes. Some better than others."

"So, you say. Yet, you don't recognize me," Jessica asserts, her face barely illuminated amidst the dimness of the basement. I fixate my gaze upon her, searching for any flicker of recognition but find none. Bewilderment clouds my thoughts – is this really all because of a slighted client?

"Perhaps you have a better memory for names than you do for faces. Does the name *Carlson* sound familiar to you?" Jessica spits the name like venom from her mouth.

"We worked with the Carlson family a year or two ago. The man thought his house was haunted by demons," I respond, only providing the basic facts.

"That man's name was Emmanuel, and he was my husband. We were married for *thirteen years*. And me? I'm the one who hired you." She takes a deep breath. "I knew your little business was phoney from the moment I saw your ad listing in the local newspaper. Your website was even more cliché, which is why I thought you'd be perfect to help wake Emmanuel out of whatever psychosis he was experiencing. You all thought you were scamming my family like you do everyone else, but I knew exactly what was happening, and I counted on it.

"Since Emmanuel refused to see a doctor or psychologist, and I refused to forcibly admit him to an institution for treatment, I indulged his delusions, instead. That boyfriend of yours lays it on thick, doesn't he? My husband hung on to every word he said like it was scripture. And then you came along with your clairvoyant powers and spewed lie after ridiculous lie about the people who lived in the house before us, and why they were haunting us. You even entertained the idea of demonic entities, and Emmanuel believed it all.

"On the night of your ritual, we sent the kids to my parents' house while we watched you do a 'clearing'. Let me tell you, that was a performance worthy of an award. When it was all over, there was peace. I felt like for the first time all year, I got my Emmanuel back. I sent you all off with thousands of dollars of my hard-earned money, but it was worth it. Emmanuel and I spent the night together, and things were finally looking up. I thought I'd tricked him into thinking the ghosts were gone, vanquished by the professional ghosthunters. But I was wrong. The next morning, I left to pick up the kids. When I came home, Emmanuel had locked himself in our bedroom, claiming that the spirits were still there and that they were 'more vengeful' than ever. I was devastated.

"A few days later, I took our youngest with me grocery shopping. The boys, Brian and Todd, were going to a friend's house. Emmanuel, obviously, had still barricaded himself in our room at home. I'd tried to get him to come out, but he just wouldn't listen to me. I had exhausted all of my options, so I was going to call the doctor and have him admitted, but I never got the chance to. When Charlotte and I came home, the house was on fire. That's when I saw the boys through the window, trapped in our bedroom with Emmanuel standing behind them. They were pounding their little fists on the window and screaming, but Emmanuel had completely lost it. He held them both tight so they couldn't escape. I watched my sons and my husband burn alive – my husband, who became even more manic after you came into our home and filled his head with even more nonsense than there already was."

I want to feel bad for Jessica, but it's hard when she has a gun pointed at me.

"I'm so sorry, I had no idea," I tell her.

"Well, of course, you didn't! How could you have known? You all just take people's money and disappear, don't you? Your sister was the only decent one among you," Jessica retorts, her frustration palpable.

"What do you mean?"

"Well, she must have stumbled upon the news of the murder-suicide and recognized the Carlson name and house. After multiple email attempts of Kinsley reaching out to me, we met for lunch and have been in contact ever since. When she temporarily rejoined the group, it was because Kinsley vowed to put an end to the tragedies and scams. With my help, we made alternative arrangements for that girl who replaced Kinsley's position, Alison I believe, freeing up a place in The Larua Group for Kinsley to rejoin.

"The Mull House job, the entire backstory – it's all a fabrication, a plan to dismantle the group. I created the pretences for gathering you all in one place, while Kinsley stayed undercover, reporting information from the inside and ensuring things ran smoothly. All she wanted was to make amends with me for her role in my family's deaths, and she thought she was doing that by getting you all out of business. But I planned on taking you all out, instead. Including Kinsley. That boy, Toby, was a complication, and although he wasn't the intended target, I had to kill him anyway. Tie up loose ends, and all that. I used the opportunity to stage my own murder, too. As soon as I had the chance, I moved his body to a disguised storage closet and hid. When I heard that you had split into groups, you made it so much easier for me. And you," Jessica pauses, a grim tone colouring her voice, "you lasted the longest. So, congratulations. Unfortunately, you've still lost the game. As your consolation prize, you get to choose where I shoot you."

The emptiness in Jessica's eyes leaves no room for doubt – she's serious as a heart attack. Even in the face of craziness, a sense of calm overcomes me. Everyone I care about is dead – Ledger, the man I thought was the love of my life; Brooklyn, my trusted friend; Sam and Toby, whose futures were cut so short. But above all, it's Kinsley who holds the ultimate power over my heart. She was my purpose, and I failed to protect her. Without purpose, life loses its meaning, and I've undoubtedly just lost mine. Maybe after what I did to Randy, my mother, and Ledger, I deserve to die, too.

And to meet my end through a gunshot, it's an ironic finale straight from the pages of a Shakespearean tragedy.

Death by a bullet is quick, a comparatively better fate

than drowning or being consumed by flames, lungs filled with smoke and soot; like how Ledger died. Soon enough, I'll meet the fate I deserve.

"So, what's it going to be?" Jessica's voice breaks through my thoughts.

The smoke slowly seeping into the basement causes my nostrils to burn, and I realize that regardless of my decision, death awaits me. My trembling finger points shakily to my heart, and Jessica adjusts her aim accordingly.

Two things happen simultaneously: Jessica collapses to the ground, and the piercing sound of a gunshot reverberates in my ears. In Jessica's place stands Kinsley, who drops a rusty fire poker on the cement floor with a *clink*. Only, it's not rust that stains the tip of the poker, but blood. A small pool of crimson begins to form beneath Jessica's head, seeping into her blonde hair. Her eyes remain open as if she might rise at any moment and finish me off.

But she won't.

It's all over now.

"Kinsley, you're safe," I whisper, relieved to see my sister alive. "Everything's going to be all right."

Her body is motionless, her face frozen, staring blankly ahead. She doesn't utter a word, and in the silence, I become aware of a sharp pain in my side. It's only when I follow her tunnel-vision gaze that I look down and see that I've been shot.

Thirty-Two

Beck & Kinsley

2006

Police officers and detectives had swarmed the Rollins household like worker bees in a hive.

It seemed as if every inch of Beck's home was being poked and prodded, with police officers and men in coats collecting things and placing them in sealed bags. They put tiny yellow cones, numbered in no particular order, on the ground near Randy's corpse. Flashes of light illuminated the room for milliseconds at a time as a female officer photographed the body, the wounds, and the blood.

Beck watched methodically as a forensic investigator had begun to measure the blood splatter surrounding Randy's body. The man had dropped to his knees and measured the length and width of each blood stain, noting the shape and size to determine the velocity of impact. The man scribbled his findings in a pocket-sized notebook and left the scene of the crime, ducking under the yellow tape at Beck's front door.

Kinsley drank a juice box and sat on the staircase, blissfully unaware of the gravity of the scene unfolding before her. Beck sat on the steps next to her, much like she had done alone earlier that night, and spoke to a young officer. She recounted the events just like her mother had told her to. Beck told the truth about Randy's abuse and about the beatings that took place that night but lied about who was holding the gun when a bullet was fired into Randy's skull.

"Listen, baby," Beck's mom had told her earlier, before the authorities arrived to investigate. "You were just trying to protect me, I know that. It's okay. You did what I didn't have the guts to do, and you shouldn't be punished for that. It's my turn to finally protect you like I should have done all these years. The police officers are going to ask you to make a statement, and they're going to ask a lot of questions. You're going to tell them the truth about Randy except for the part where you shoot the gun. Instead of *you* shooting it, we're going to say that it was me. I'm the one who snatched the gun from him and shot him in self-defence. And you'll say that you saw the whole thing unravel."

"But you didn't shoot the gun," Beck protested.

"Yes, I did. I shot the gun. I killed Randy. I shot him, it was me. Say it with me, Mommy shot Randy. Mommy shot Randy."

Beck had started to cry.

"*Please*, Beck. Say it. Mommy shot Randy."

"Mommy… Mommy shot Randy."

Beck's Mom kissed her on the forehead and hugged her tighter than she ever had before.

"Good girl. I love you so much. That's the truth from now on, okay? Don't ever tell anyone otherwise, not the police, not even Kinsley. This is the story you have to tell to live the life you deserve. I'm sorry I didn't protect you, I'm so, so sorry." Tears filled Beck's mother's eyes, but she quickly wiped them with her sleeve.

After Beck and her mother's heart-to-heart, the police stormed into their house with shields and guns after someone reported hearing a gunshot from their residence. Beck's mother had put her hands in the air and backed away from her daughter.

Soon after, Beck watched as the police arrested her mother and ushered her outside and into the back of a cruiser like they do in the movies.

In the aftermath of the shooting, Beck did as her mother instructed and told the police officer a story that corroborated her mother's statement. For hours, the house was filled to the brim with officers, detectives, social workers, and later, extended family members. Beck and Kinsley were not alone for a moment during the following forty-eight hours, but Beck felt alone anyway.

The first night without her mom, Beck could not sleep. She felt like an abandoned house, forgotten and lost to time, and so that's what Beck would think about as she tried to fall asleep.

In this house, Beck imagined that the windows were boarded up with rusted nails and splintered wood, and cobwebs clung to every dusty corner. Floorboards creaked with each step and a musty odour permeated each room. Headless dolls and lifeless teddy bears littered the hardwood, left behind by a child who had lost their innocence. Beck felt like she was in a place like this, where no one had lived for years – a place where emotions had been left to rot and decay and wither away like flowers in an abandoned garden.

The emptiness inside her was like this abandoned house, a place where there was once innocence and love, but was now a desolate and lonely husk, filled with nothing but the memories of what once was.

Thirty-Three

Beck

2019

My eyes burn from the blinding lights above me.

For a moment, I think I might be dead, but then I realize that people like me don't go to Heaven, so I must be alive. Either that or Hell is much nicer than people believe. I swallow my disappointment and try to keep my eyes open but the light stings too much. My brain is a puddle of mush and exhaustion that keeps me from fully waking. Eventually, I stop trying and am lulled back to the safety of sleep, the darkness enveloping every corner of my being.

***

The next time I wake up, there's a man in the room.

I'm able to open my eyes for a minute before the light becomes unbearable again. With my eyes closed, I become aware of my other senses. The air is cool and dry. A strong smell – is that rubbing alcohol? – lingers in my nostrils. There are also many sounds; the man's voice as he hums some indistinguishable tune to himself, his heavy footsteps on the linoleum tile, and the sound of rustling papers around. But there's one sound I don't recognize, and after thinking about it for a while, though I'm not sure how long exactly, I come to the realization that it's a hospital machine.

I'm in a hospital.

I open my eyes and shoot straight up out of the narrow bed, but a shooting pain in my stomach keeps me from getting more than half upright. I fall back to the firm cushion of the mattress. My limbs are heavy and unresponsive as if they don't belong to me. I look around frantically, and the machine I'd heard, the heart rate monitor, beeps incessantly. My breathing becomes shallow and rapid, and my brain fogs with a confused haze.

"Miss Rollins," the man says, appearing in my field of view. "It's okay, take deep breaths. I'm going to get the doctor, okay?"

He presses a button on the wall that makes a buzzing noise. I just want all the noise to stop.

"My name is Jerome; I've been the RN taking care of you this past week. You were in rough shape, but it's a good sign that you're awake now."

"A week?" I ask. My voice is hoarse, and I sound like a frog croaking. I slowly stop hyperventilating but my difficulty breathing isn't going away.

"Try not to speak just yet. You had pretty bad smoke inhalation from the fire." That's right, the fire at Mull House. The fire that Jessica set after she killed everyone.

"…lack of oxygen to the brain," Jerome says. He keeps talking but I've mentally checked-out, trying to remember the events as they unfolded.

Jessica set the fire when she locked Ledger in the room, and I left him there. *Shit*, I really left him to die. What kind of a person does that? I compartmentalize the decision and the feelings that come with it for the moment because my head hurts too much to comprehend my decision.

Then…then what?

I went to the basement looking for Kinsley and found Jessica instead. She had a gun and was going to kill me to avenge the deaths of her family. And then Kinsley, who I thought was dead, came out of nowhere and killed her.

And then I woke up here.

"The patient is out of the coma, Dr. Gupta, but she appears to be phasing in and out of consciousness. Elevated heart rate and BP."

I look to my left and see the nurse conversing with a new person. A woman who looks to be in her forties.

"Thank you, Jerome. I'll take it from here."

The doctor, clad in white scrubs, walks in my direction and sets her clipboard down at the foot of my bed. She begins to examine the various machines and wires attached to my body.

"Miss Rollins, I – may I call you Beck?" I nod. "Beck, how are you feeling?"

I take Jerome's advice and refrain from speaking, shaking my head in response.

"That is to be expected. Your body has been through a lot this past week. Thankfully, the gunshot grazed the left side of your abdomen, so there was minimal damage on that front. Another inch of two, though, and the bullet might have penetrated major organs. You are quite lucky, Beck."

Okay, so I was shot. I vaguely remember that now, hearing a gunshot after Kinsley and Jessica fought and then passing out.

"The damage from smoke inhalation is the real concern. The building was a historic one, constructed with wood and older, more flammable materials. After the initial fire was set, it did not take long for the flames to travel to every inch of that house. That is what the fire captain on the scene said, at least. Smoke inhalation such as this can cause seizures, confusion, loss of mental faculties, or in your case, a coma. It is impossible to say just how intense the long-term side effects of this will be, but we will work with you every step of the way. The largest obstacle to overcome was emerging from your coma, and so hopefully it is onward and upward from here."

I nod my head in understanding.

"I am going to provide you with a pen and pad so that you can communicate more effectively for the time being. Your vocal cords will heal in time, but it is best not to risk straining them for now." The doctor shows me a notebook and two pens, before placing them all on my bedside table. "You can write down anything you want or need, and my team or I will assist you to the best of our abilities. Do you have any questions?"

I try to process the information she's giving me, but it's like I really do have a fog in my brain. The more I think about it, the more my mind feels like a maze, with no clear path to follow. The confusion only adds to the mental fog, as if they're feeding off each other in some parasitic dynamic. One question cuts through the haze, though, and distress surges through every inch of my body for not thinking to ask it sooner.

I point to the notebook and pen, and the doctor lays them on my lap. I open the cover and let my pen fly furiously across the lined paper.

WHERE IS MY SISTER ?

"I – I apologize, but it is not my place. The detectives will tell you everything when you feel comfortable and competent enough to speak with them."

She gives me a curt smile and avoids eye contact as she abruptly leaves the room, her head facing the floor.

Thirty-Four

Beck

2019

THREE DAYS LATER

I'm watching the local news on one of those puny square T.V. screens screwed into the top corner of the room. The headline **MULL HOUSE MASSACRE** is pasted over the bottom of the screen as a reporter stands outside the charred remnants of Mull

House. I try to watch the report, but my neck hurts from craning my head so much to the right and I mentally curse whoever designed this room from hell.

"Miss Rollins?"

There's a knock at the door but it opens before I can respond.

I roll my eyes and sit up in bed, wincing when my body reacts to my sudden movement.

The nurse, Jerome, enters my room with two police officers behind him. My heart seizes in my chest and my breaths become shallow.

"Is now a good time?"

"Well, I'm not dead or in a coma, so it's about as good a time as we're going to get, I guess." Neither the male nor the female cop laughs, and my attempt at a joke lands flat. My weak voice only makes the attempt more pathetic. As he's leaving the room, Jerome smiles, though. He closes the door quietly behind him.

"Miss Rollins," the man says.

"Please, just call me Beck."

"Okay, Beck. My name is Detective Walker, and this is my partner, Officer Larson. Before we begin, please state your full legal name, age, and date of birth for the record."

"Rebecca Ainsley Rollins. I'm twenty-five years old. My

birthday is August 11th, 1993."

"Thank you. If you're willing and able, we'd like to take a statement from you regarding the incident at Mull House, detailing your account of events."

"All right."

I wait for one of them to say something, but an awkward quietness lingers thick in the room. Finally, the woman, Officer Larson, breaks the silence.

"The floor is yours. We don't have any initial questions for you right now, but we do need you to recount the events to the best of your ability. Then we'll have some questions."

"I have a question before we start."

"Yes?"

"Where is my sister, Kinsley? The doctors and nurses won't tell me what happened because they say it's not their place. I've assumed, then, that it's *your* place. So, tell me, where is my sister?"

Not knowing anything about Kinsley's whereabouts for the last three days has been agonizing, like the way a mother feels when separated from her child. I can hardly sleep, and my mind keeps racing whenever I try. I can't stand the unknown and the perpetual unease that accompanies it.

The police officers look at each other, mirroring blank expressions.

"Your sister was arrested for one count of murder in the second degree following the statement she provided to officers on the scene after you both were rescued."

The few pieces I have left of my heart wither away. This cannot be happening, not to Kinsley.

"She was saving me!" I yell. My throat instantly burns and I regret the sudden increase in volume.

"Beck, please –"

"It was self-defence! That psycho would have killed me if it weren't for my sister, how fucking blind are you? She had a gun and everything!" I sit up in my hospital bed, waving my arms around hysterically trying to prove my point.

"Hey, watch your language," the male officer warns.

"I got this," the woman says quietly.

"Beck," she continues, "I know how difficult this must be for you, but Kinsley needs your help right now. As both a victim and a witness in this investigation, we need you to give a statement. Every piece of information helps."

I can't even muster a breath right now, let alone give a statement that will help determine my sister's fate. But it's exactly because of Kinsley that I force myself to do this.

I choose my next words, and all the words after that, carefully.

"As I'm sure you've gathered, the reason we went to

Nova Scotia is that we have – we had – a small business called The Larua Group. People would hire us to investigate their houses with our ghost-hunting equipment. Some clients hired us as a joke or a gag, and for others who believed their house was haunted, well, we would investigate their houses. A woman calling herself Jessica Mull propositioned us, and even though we were in Ontario, we took the job because she offered us a substantial commission. She covered our travel expenses, and gas, and opened the doors of Mull House for us to stay, free of charge.

"So, we travelled to Nova Scotia together. It took about two days to drive here from Southern Ontario. When we arrived at Mull House, Jessica was warm and inviting. She had rooms prepared for us and fed us meals. On the first day, we were tired from the journey, so we rested. We didn't leave the property, but some of us went exploring around the house. The next day, we decided to go out and do some touring around the town of Mulgrave. We drove around, went to a convenience store, and spent most of the day at the waterfront."

Ledger shattered my heart at the waterfront, but I don't tell them that. The last thing I need is for them to have probable cause to expand their investigation into me as a suspect in Ledger's murder. Right now, Kinsley's fate is hanging in the balance, and I don't have time to feel guilty about my role in

Ledger's death.

"The group of us spent an hour or so there," I continue, "but left when it began to rain. We went back to Mull House and Jessica ordered food from the diner near the town limits. We ate together and everything seemed normal until there were unexplained sounds and footsteps, which is the sort of thing Jessica complained about to begin with. When we decided to formally begin the investigation, every piece of equipment was either broken or malfunctioned. Sam was heartbroken about that."

I pause and take a shaky breath, willing myself not to cry. Sam loved our equipment. He helped design and manufacture things like our EMF detector and Ghost Box. Aside from Toby, those devices were his pride and joy. He loved to create and invent new things. But Sam is gone, and so is Toby, who will never conduct another interview or write an expose again. Brooklyn will never buy another pair of shoes or go on a shopping spree again, either. Everyone is gone except me and Kinsley, and she's as good as gone if she's found guilty and incarcerated in another province. There is a gaping hole in my chest at the thought of Kinsley being in jail because of me, a fate just like our mother's.

A lone tear escapes my tear ducts and I swiftly wipe it away.

"I guess I should also mention that Sam's fiancé, Toby, didn't know about The Larua Group or Sam's involvement in it. Sam felt awful about lying to Toby, but he continued working with us because of the easy income and his friendship with Ledger. The only way Sam agreed to come with us on this job was if Toby could come, so Ledger came up with the idea of disguising the gig as a tourism ghost experience. Toby was under the impression that we were going on a vacation to a seaside town and staying in a haunted house where we would pay to experience these ghosts.

"When we started the investigation, masked as the ghost experience to Toby, we all went upstairs while Jessica offered to stay with Toby in the sitting room. Toby wasn't into ghosts or anything horror-related, so it all seemed like it was going to work out. But, as I said, the equipment was somehow broken, and we went back downstairs to tell them about it. When we got to the main floor, though, Jessica and Toby were dead. Well, we thought Jessica was dead at the time. Sam was devastated and sat next to Toby. He held his body and just... sat there.

"We realized the danger we were in and started to freak out. Once we discovered that the front doors were locked, we split off into groups to find an exit. Ledger and Brooklyn went upstairs, and Kinsley and I took the main floor. Sam was in shock, and he wouldn't leave Toby, so we let him stay with the bodies. The next thing I know, Kinsley and I were separated, I found Brooklyn's dead body, and when I went downstairs in search of my sister, the bodies in the parlour were gone, and so was Sam."

I pause to catch my breath, having sped through the last few sentences and glazing over the part where I abandoned Ledger in the burning playroom. The detectives scribble ferociously in their notepads, not missing a beat. Once I catch my breath, I try to continue the story, but the words won't leave my mouth – because this is the part after I lost Kinsley.

I'm the one who dragged her into The Larua Group in the first place when she explicitly told me time and time again that she didn't feel good about scamming clients. But I forced her into it anyway. I should have listened to her; I should have respected her wishes and prioritized her well-being over the group. I failed to protect my baby sister and if Kinsley goes away for this… I'll never forgive myself.

The guilt swallows me in a whirlpool, the anchor of my ineptitude and selfishness dragging me down, down, down, until I've sunk into the abyss.

"Beck?"

The woman's voice is a distant echo. She and her partner murmur something and call for the doctor.

Every breath is shallow, as if my lungs are constricted.

Every thought is more incoherent than the last, dancing about my mind in a frenzied waltz.

Every tear that slides down my cheek is a reminder that I am derelict. A disappointment.

The nurse, Jerome, enters my room and ushers the police officers out. After he closes the door, I collapse into a trembling mess. Sobbing so hard that I dry-heave and cry so much that I run out of tears.

"I'm awful, I'm- I'm a terrible si- sister."

"You're not awful. Try to take some deep breaths," Jerome says. He talks me through a deep breathing exercise that doesn't help in the slightest.

"She went to jail… for me. They bo- both went to jail be- *because of me*!"

Jerome must realize that he's in over his head and pages for another nurse or a doctor. His movements are blurred like I'm seeing through a kaleidoscope. My vision becomes so hazy that all I see are shapes and blobs.

My body and my mind cannot take anymore, every inch of me is exhausted. Finally, my head hits the pillow and I'm at peace.

Thirty-Five

Beck

2019

I stay in the hospital for another week and undergo a psych evaluation. I'm diagnosed with post-traumatic stress disorder, which doesn't surprise me as much as it should. I've been no stranger to trauma, and instead of facing it, I've been on the run from it for years.

I guess it's finally caught up to me.

***

I pack up a few belongings from my hospital room before I'm formally discharged. They've prescribed me anxiety medication to take once daily and strongly recommended seeing a therapist to address my traumas. While I'm certain that I'll comply with the medication regimen, the prospect of opening up about my past feels daunting. I'm not sure that I'm ready to confide in anyone, or if I ever will be.

How did I ever want to be a psychologist when I refuse to even see one myself?

The discharge process goes by in a slow blur. Jerome, the kind nurse who took care of me, gives me a warm hug and orders me a drive to the airport through a rideshare app.

***

A few hours later, I land in Toronto and make arrangements for a taxi to drive me home. Smog fills the city air, quickly reminding me of the reprieve of salty breeze and fresh Nova Scotian air.

From the outside, our apartment building is unchanged,

but as I trudge my way up the stairs to my apartment and open the door, the space is different. It's dark and deathly quiet, and even after I switch the lights on, there's something wrong about being in this apartment without Ledger.

Ledger's things are still here, waiting for an owner that will never return – and I'm responsible for that. I'm the reason he won't come home; I'm the reason that he and that other woman's baby will grow up without a genuine father, just like I did.

Kinsley suffered from my actions, too. She grew up without a father figure, however flawed he might have been, and without a mother as well. It's my fault that my mother ended up in jail, and it's my fault Kinsley's in prison, too. Both of them were incarcerated while protecting me, and I didn't deserve it.

I'm a monster.

I'm a fucking monster.

***

Kinsley.

Mom.

Randy.

Ledger.

Brooklyn.

Sam.

Toby.

Every night, as I lay sleeplessly in bed, I force myself to say their names over and over again, a guilt-ridden ritual. I repeat the sequence of names like a prayer or a chant, pronouncing each syllable. With every whispered name, their faces flash before my eyes, vividly resurrected by my guilt and remorse. I don't do it to make me remember what I've done, because I'll never let myself forget that until the day I die. No, it's a way to remind myself of how much pain and suffering I have caused to the people in my life.

Kinsley.

Mom.

Randy.

Ledger.

Brooklyn.

Sam.

Toby.

And repeat.

***

Sometimes, while I drown in the depths of my guilt and self-pity, I catch myself thinking about the Carlson family – because

Jessica – Linda Carlson – was wrong about me.

In the basement of Mull House, right before Linda broke into her cliché villainous monologue, there was a look in her eyes, a familiarity that I'd seen somewhere before. It was the stained blood on her face that confirmed my suspicions, though. During the Carlson case, her husband cut himself with a knife, causing blood to splatter onto her face. I can't say for certain if it was an accidental injury, but the end result was the same: Emmanuel Carlson lost his index finger in their family kitchen during our initial Larua Group meeting. After seeing the blood on her sharp cheekbones, I knew then and there that it was Linda Carlson who stood before me.

The reality is that long before Mull House, I'd come across the news of the murder-suicide, and I recognized the Carlson family from the photographs news outlets used to accompany their story. My initial reaction was to fear legal recourse from Linda Carlson, but it never came. Eventually, the *Carlson Family Murder-Suicide* became old news – like most tragic events today, one family's nightmare was overshadowed and replaced with a newer, more sensational tragic event.

I'd be lying if I said I wasn't relieved when the situation faded into oblivion, because a week or two after the news outlets stopped reporting on the tragedy, Linda Carlson and her family became a distant memory, and I never gave them a second thought.

***

Each morning is the same, simultaneously mundane absence and presence of routine. I usually start the day at noon, sometimes earlier, but mostly later. I drag myself out of bed to the kitchen and take my anxiety pill with a sip of water. Then I go back into bed. I don't fall back asleep, at least not right away. I just exist.

The police have called me and left a message wanting to schedule a follow-up interview over video call so that I can complete my witness statement. I deleted the voicemail. I've said all I have to say for now.

I haven't showered in four days, maybe five. I feel disgusting but I can't bring myself to do anything about it. My hair is matted into a messy bun that is anything but stylish, and my face is sunken and pale like a corpse from a Tim Burton film. Ledger and I used to love watching his movies, especially around Halloween. But there'll be no spooky movie marathon this year, and probably for a while after.

The last thing I need in my life right now is more ghosts.

Thirty-Six

Beck

2019

I twitch in my sleep and wake up with a jolt that shakes both my whole body and the wooden bed frame. Someone is knocking at the door.

I roll over to my side and put a pillow over my exposed ear to block out the sound and wait it out. The pillow does nothing to aid me, and the knocking continues – it's probably the police doing a wellness check. If they want to come in then they can break down the goddamn door, because I'm sure as hell not opening it for them.

The incessant knocking ceases and the now-foreign feeling of relief washes over me. On the nightstand next to me, my phone buzzes. When I pick it up and read the message, my eyes widen, and I do a double take.

SAM: it's me. open the door beck

I stare at the screen with what must be the most dumbfounded look a person can have. Sam is dead. He's gone, just like everyone else. It's just me, Kinsley, and her dog who came out of Mull House alive, and only me who came home after it all. Someone is playing a cruel prank on me.

The continue starts up again and I growl as I get out of bed and stomp to the entryway and open the front door. A man stands in the hallway with his back to the door.

"I don't know what kind of sick game you think you're playing but cut it the hell out."

He turns around and my knees turn to gelatin.

"Hey, Beck."

It's Sam, his kind and beautiful brown eyes staring right

at me.

"But, you, I thought you were –"

"Can I come inside?"

I gesture for him to come inside, my cheeks burning with embarrassment at the state of my apartment. The lights are off, the curtains are drawn shut, and dirty laundry is littered on the floor. We walk into the living room, where a few weeks prior, we had all sat to discuss the Mull House job. The thoughts send a shiver down my spine.

"Beck, are you okay?" Sam asks, his concern breaking through. "That's a dumb question, neither of us is freaking okay."

"You've got that right."

"Seriously though, as soon as I was able, I went to the hospital to visit you, but they said you had already been discharged. What happened?"

"Why don't you tell me what the hell happened to you? One minute you're in the room with, *you know*, and the next you've all disappeared. I feared the worst and thought you had died too."

"I was devastated about Toby. I still am, obviously. When you all split into groups, I couldn't do anything but sit with him and cry. I felt so guilty that the last things I said to him were hurtful. Not long after that, I realized the danger I was in staying down there alone. I gave Toby one last kiss and got up to find you. But something grabbed my ankle and I fell forward on the floor."

"The bang," I recall. "Kinsley and I heard a noise but didn't know what it was."

"Yeah, that was me. Jessica – Linda, I mean – grabbed me. Obviously, I was shocked to see that she wasn't, you know, dead. But I was so shocked that I couldn't find my voice. I couldn't scream. I kicked and thrashed to be free from her grasp and accidentally hooved her in the face. That set her back a bit, so I took off running and instead of fighting or trying to warn you, I was a coward. I hid in the dumbwaiter in the kitchen and waited the whole thing out. Well, until the smoke eventually drew me out of my hiding place. But by then, firefighters were barging in, forcing the front door open. I'm so sorry I didn't help you, Beck."

Without hesitation, I lean forward and give Sam a hug.

"Sorry, I'm all gross and sweaty," I say, self-conscious over my personal hygiene, which plummeted following my stay at the hospital. "Probably not the best person to hug right now."

"I'd rather you gross and sweaty and *alive* than not here at all."

Together, we piece together a theory with the facts we already have: while we were all upstairs, Linda killed Toby and staged her own death. After we discovered the bodies and split up, Linda – having hidden Toby's body – lurked in secret, intending to pick us off one by one. Linda eliminated Ledger by locking him in the playroom, which she ignited so that she could reach Brooklyn. After killing Brooklyn, she pursued Kinsley and me, saving me for last.

As Sam finishes his account, I share my own perspective from that night, including the basement showdown and Linda's motives for targeting us. We delve into Linda's grief, trying to understand her need for revenge after the loss of her children, taken from her by the man she loved. When you're grieving, you desperately search for someone to hold accountable – and whether we deserved the blame or not, Linda held The Larua Group accountable.

"I feel awful about her family, but at the same time, death doesn't cancel out death."

"I think she just wanted to feel like she had some control after everything that happened to her and her kids. Two of her children were killed, taken from her by the man she loved. She helplessly watched outside the house through the window and couldn't do anything about it until it was too late."

"Did she have other children?" he asks. "You said two of her kids were killed. Were there more?"

"Now that you mention it, I'm not sure. I think there

was a third child, the youngest one, but Linda didn't go into depth on that." My brain has been in a depressive haze, my body going through the motions like a robot. I'm not sure if my lack of knowledge is really a lack of memory. My head aches from trying to remember.

"We don't have to keep talking about Mull House if you don't want to. It's still fresh for both of us and, correct me if I'm wrong, but right now, we're both hot messes who lost their partners." Sam starts to cry but laughs through the tears. "See? A hot mess."

The chuckle that comes from my mouth surprises me. It's subtle, but it happened.

"Maybe we could just hang out together if that's fine with you."

Sam squeezes my hand, and it's the happiest I've felt in weeks.

"I would love nothing more."

At this moment, my laugh, small and subtle as it was, is a fragile sign that maybe, just maybe, healing can be found in each other's presence.

Thirty-Seven

Beck

2019

With Sam's support, I'm finally able to provide the police in
Nova Scotia with a full statement.

After we were both done, Sam contacted an old friend
from high school, Nina Hobbes, who has a small law firm. He
initially hired Nina for a consultation to assess whether or not

the police had grounds to investigate or charge us for our role in The Larua Group. After questioning us relentlessly about every aspect of The Larua Group, Mull House, and the Carlson murder-suicide, Nina concludes that we haven't *technically* broken any laws. We provided a service, our clients paid for it, and we delivered as promised. Despite the bullshit nature of the service itself, our customers were aware of what they were getting into. From a legal standpoint, our actions and business fall on the right side of the law – morally, not so much.

As for our involvement in the Carlson family murder-suicide, Nina asserts that there's no concrete evidence connecting us to the family that would be admissible in court, if the case even got that far in the first place.

By all legal accounts, Sam and I are in the clear. On many other fronts, though, there's still much that needs to be resolved.

Kinsley is still facing charges of manslaughter in Nova Scotia, but Nina is working tirelessly to have them dropped. It brings me some relief knowing that we're taking steps to free my sister, but my mind won't ease completely until she's back home, safe where she belongs.

Sam continues to mourn the loss of Toby, the love of his life, and Ledger, one of his closest friends. In my own way, I find myself grieving for Ledger, too. Not so much for him as an individual, as harsh as it might sound, but for the vision I had of our relationship and the future we could have had together; the future that I was so safe and secure in.

Now, there's nothing safe or secure about my life, but despite this, I can't help but feel like better days are coming. I undoubtedly hit rock bottom in the weeks following Mull House, which means the only direction I can go from here on out is upward.

Thirty-Eight

Kinsley

2019

The Mull House operation was my idea.

After hearing about the Carlson family murder-suicide on the local news and recognizing the surname, I sobbed in front of the TV. I grew up without a mom, but those kids won't ever grow up at all. Those two little boys were robbed of their lives at the hands of their father, who was in all likelihood, experiencing some sort of psychological break. The Larua Group was the spark that set their lives on fire, killing innocent people. They took advantage of an unwell man and a desperate wife, and their children were caught in the crosshairs.

Worst of all, I was a part of it.

That same day, I'd reached out to Linda Carlson over email and expressed my condolences. She basically told me to shove my thoughts and prayers where the sun doesn't shine. And how could I blame her? I was in the group that helped kill her family.

I tried to separate myself from the group. I told myself I was different, that I wasn't one of them. Linda Carlson recognized this and called me on it. And she was right – I was a member of The Larua Group, and eventually, I came to accept that. But with that acceptance came responsibility and the dedication to become a better person, to right the wrongs I'd contributed to. So, I quit the group for good and put flowers on the Carlson graves as often as I could; I anonymously donated to the fundraising campaign for Linda and her only living child, set up by Linda's parents; and I even found the new, temporary Carlson address and delivered a homemade peach cobbler to her porch.

None of this made up for what I'd done, though. It helped to *feel* like I was helping, but it was surface-level, meaningless acts of service. I wanted to do something that counts, and a year later, when my perception of Beck permanently changed, I understood what Linda felt when I contacted her. But the difference is that Beck didn't seem sorry at all. She didn't even have the decency to tell me the truth about how our childhood had been uprooted and why the course of our lives was altered that night, let alone apologize.

That's right – I know Beck is the one who killed Randy, and I've known the truth for two years.

Beck always talks about protecting me, her naïve, sweet, fragile little sister, but it backfired; she didn't protect me. She used lies as a shelter, a hiding place to protect me from the harsh truth surrounding Randy's death. But those lies were like using a band-aid to treat a stab wound, and eventually, the wound gaped open.

Internally, I held so much resentment towards my sister. but being the non-confrontational, *sweet* little sister, I never said a word. I just smiled and bared it, because I'd already lost my mother – and I didn't want to lose the only family I had left.

Before discovering Beck's betrayal, I grieved for Linda and sympathized with her tragedy. But after I found the letter that revealed the truth about Randy's death, I empathized with

Linda. And so, a year later, I reached out to her via email once again. This time, I took accountability for my role in the deaths of her family.

When Linda and I first met up at the site of the Carlson house, which was transformed into a dilapidated pile of soot and burnt memories, I made multiple offers about how I could help her, and finally make amends. Her path toward peace wasn't exactly peaceful, though. It was vengeful – only, I didn't know it at the time.

Linda and I corresponded for months, meeting at various locations around the city for coffee or a walk in the park, and we'd brainstorm.

"Just know that even though I'm working with you now, it doesn't mean I forgive you for what you did," Linda had said in one of our first meetings. We'd decided to meet up at a park with a picnic area, and we each brought something to eat for lunch. I opted for my daily Frappuccino and chocolate-dipped donut while Linda brought fruit, some pieces having white fuzz to mark their age.

"As far as I'm concerned, you're just as guilty as the others except for your demonstration of remorse."

"I know how hard it must be to work with me and not against me, but I promise, I'm on your side. I just want to help you heal."

After plenty of back and forth, I finally came up with the brilliant idea for Mull House.

"You just bought a new home, right?" I asked, knowing the Carlson family home had burnt to a crisp with her husband and sons inside.

"We're in escrow right now, but yes. I've decided to relocate to Nova Scotia and start over under a new name. Jessica Mull."

"What if we use that new name and house to hire The Larua Group for a Clearing so big that they couldn't possibly refuse?"

"But would they all travel to the East Coast for that? If they're in this group to make quick cash, then they can't have that much money to their names."

She'd made a fair point.

"Yeah, that's true. And this might be an awful idea, especially since it would be costing *you* money, but you did get a payout from your home and life insurance," I said, my voice trailing off before I finished the suggestion.

Linda sat with the implication and didn't speak for a minute.

"I'm sorry, I knew that was probably a bad idea," I continued, instantly feeling guilty for even mentioning the insurance payout from her husband's death.

"No, no," she said. "I like it. I'd be using the money that came from their deaths to avenge their deaths. Other than buying a new house and relocating, I can't see a more fitting use of the funds. But you're right, I don't want to forfeit too much money. How about, I pay for their travel expenses and accommodations, which shouldn't be more than a few thousand dollars. I tease them with their payout, dangling it like a carrot in front of a horse, but won't ever actually have to pay it."

"That's perfect. None of them believe in the supernatural, but we'll scare them so badly that they'll become believers. They'll never want to do another job again, and they'll be out of business by the time we're through with them," I say. I was thinking of how scary pyrotechnics and illusions would be in a creepy mansion, but Linda had other ideas.

"… Or we could put them down instead?"

"You don't mean to be suggesting…"

Linda's silence and blank expression answered my question for her.

"My heart is broken. I am broken. This pain, this grief, has devoured my capability for happiness and optimism. The laughter and chaos that once filled our home, the small hands that touched everything, is gone. It's all gone. My boys, my sweet boys. I'm so overwhelmed by this unrelenting darkness; it's eaten me whole. And the worst part is that I'm still alive. No parent should have to bury their child, it's supposed to be the other way around. Every beat of my broken, shattered heart reminds me of the fact that I'm alive and they're not. Listen, I've never been a particularly violent person, but this… this has irrevocably changed me. How can I go back to PTA meetings, or attend book club on Sundays and cook meatloaf on Mondays? How can I go on living my life knowing that my boys and my poor husband are rotting in a graveyard six feet under!"

Linda slammed her fists on the wooden picnic bench with a *smack*, drawing the attention of multiple passersby.

"I don't sleep anymore. I take prescription sleep medication and yet I still don't sleep. All I can do is imagine these vivid, horrible scenes of torturing those responsible for my family's deaths, their faces marked by the heartlessness that shattered my world. When sleep finally catches me, I dream of confronting them, of unleashing the rage that engulfs me. Throughout my days, I hear my own whispered promises of revenge that weigh on my conscience, blurring the line between right and wrong. But I don't think there is a line anymore. It certainly isn't right for that group of yours to be scamming people for a living and making off like bandits, but it happens. It isn't right that my husband, who wasn't in his right mind, killed himself and our sons trying to protect them all from the demons he claimed haunted him, but that happened, too. And it's not right that I'm left alone, a widow tasked with raising my youngest child when I can't even bring myself to eat most days, but that happens, every day.

"If these things can happen, then why should I act as if there's some higher moral authority governing the world? Why can't I decide what's right and wrong for myself? Well, I've decided that I can and I am. It's wrong that my family died, and if righting that wrong costs the lives of those responsible, then I'm perfectly fine living with that."

Even today, I clearly remember tearing up after Linda's speech because I'd never heard something so raw, so real. And especially after finding out about Mom and Beck's cover-up, the idea of morality, of ethical duty, struck a chord with me.

"I'll do whatever it takes to deliver justice to you. Anything but *that*." I couldn't even bring myself to say the word.

"You're right, it was a silly suggestion –"

"But you're on board for the initial idea we discussed, right?" I asked.

"Yes, we'll put them out of business. We'll put on a show that scares them and beat them at their own game. It's a plan."

What I didn't know at the time was that it was a plan that Linda wouldn't stick to.

Thirty-Nine

Offering Condolences – E-mail Thread

2017-2018

from: **Kinsley Rollins** <kinsleyr0llins77@yahoo.com>
to: lindajanecarlson_1981@hotmail.com
date: Sat, June 3, 2017, at 11:20 AM
subject: Offering Condolences

Dear Mrs. Linda Carlson,

My name is Kinsley Rollins, and I want to offer you my most sincere condolences on the loss of your husband and children. I can't even imagine what you must be feeling, My heart breaks for you. I did not know your husband and sons, but I'm sure that they were such wonderful people, and they will always be remembered with love and fondness.

Please know that you are in my thoughts and my heart. I hope you find peace, comfort, and strength.

Sincerely,
Kinsley Rollins

---

from: **Linda Carlson** <lindajanecarlson_1981@hotmail.com>
to: kinsleyr0llins77@yahoo.com
date: Sun, June 4, 2017, at 3:12 PM
subject: Re: Offering Condolences

I know who you are and what you and your group did to my family. You are horrible people and make me sick. Your thoughts & prayers are not accepted, welcomed, or wanted. Do not contact me again.

---

from: **Kinsley Rollins** <kinsleyr0llins77@yahoo.com>
to: lindajanecarlson_1981@hotmail.com
date: Sat, June 4, 2017, at 6:30 PM
subject: Re: Offering Condolences

Linda,

Please know that I am no longer a member of The Larua Group. After the tragedy your family faced, I quit – I do not condone their actions and the way they make a living. Like you, they also make me sick, especially their group leader. Linda, I am not looking to cause you any harm, but instead to offer you my support and words of comfort.

I do hope that you'll see me as the good, honest person that I am, even if I made the mistake of being in the wrong place, at the wrong time, with the wrong group of people.

Best,

Kinsley Rollins

---

from: **Linda Carlson**

< lindajanecarlson_1981@hotmail.com>

to: kinsleyr0llins77@yahoo.com

date: Friday, June 9, 2017, at 1:54 AM

subject: Re: Offering Condolences

I am not interested in feeding your ego and mending your guilty conscience. You deserve to feel every ounce of guilt, every inkling of pain, because you caused mine in the first place. I want you to know that I am a widow at 36 years old. Neither of my sons lived past the age of 10 years old. My baby daughter will grow up never having known her father and brothers. I will raise her alone. Do not pretend that you are not a part of this, because you are. If you are looking for my forgiveness or compassion, you need to look in the mirror. You are no saint, Kinsley Rollins. You are not innocent in this. But my children were.

This is the last time I will say this: do not contact me again, or I will be taking action against you.

---

from: **Kinsley Rollins** <kinsleyr0llins77@yahoo.com>
to: lindajanecarlson_1981@hotmail.com
date: Sat, May 5, 2018, at 8:47 PM
subject: You Were Right

Dear Linda,

I know I'm the last person you want to hear from right now, but I'm writing to tell you that you were right. I did an awful thing by participating in The Larua Group and I regret my role in your family's deaths every day. But you already know about my guilt. What you don't know is that The Larua Group continues to operate and are profiting from the scamming of innocent people. They have no guilt or remorse; not even my sister feels bad, though I hate to say it.

If you ever want my assistance in filing charges against the group, I will help testify against them, even if it incriminates me, too. I want to make amends for my past actions and would love to help you by any means necessary.

Hope you're well,
Kinsley Rollins

from: **Linda Carlson**

< lindajanecarlson_1981@hotmail.com>

to: kinsleyr0llins77@yahoo.com

date: Sun, May 6, 2018, at 1:54 AM

subject: Re: You Were Right

Meet me where it happened tomorrow at noon

from: **Linda Carlson**

Forty

Kinsley

2019

THREE MONTHS LATER

I help Beck move the last of her boxes into our new loft, sweat beading down my forehead. God, this woman has a lot of stuff.

"Hey, Kins?" Beck shouts from the kitchen.

"Yeah?"

"I'm going to head over to the bank. I have a quick consult to talk about my financial options for starting school next year. You'll be okay unpacking here until I'm back?"

"Yeah," I say, smiling. "As long as you bring home Chinese food."

"Of course," she promises with a laugh.

Beck leaves, and I'm left alone in a sea of cardboard boxes and bubble wrap.

The coast is clear.

I dig through the box nearest to me, one filled with a bulky DVD/VHS player and easily a hundred DVD cases. I open every case and throw them back in when it proves fruitless. The next box is full of clothes, messily tossed together like they were fresh out of the laundry. At least I don't have to worry about putting anything back exactly the way it was. I dig my hand through the clothes until I feel a piece of paper and adrenaline rushes through me. Yanking my hand out of the box, I retrieve a week-old receipt for Beck's coffee order.

It's not what I'm looking for, so I crumple it up into a ball, bound tight like my nerves.

I move on to the next box and the next, going through each one less methodically than the last, but ultimately coming up with nothing. Hauling over the last box, it drops with a *thud* from my hands, books spilling onto the laminate. As if by some divine intervention, there's a foreign object sticking out of one of the fallen books; I pluck it out with my index finger and thumb and my body releases its tension.

I sit down on the floor, open the letter, and lay the creased paper on my lap.

The first time I found this letter, I didn't have adequate time to read it. Not for me, at least. It takes me longer to read things than most people, and even though I've gotten better since I was a kid, I like to double and triple-read things to make sure I'm understanding the words on the page. And the words on this page are worth every read-through.

A few years ago, I used a spare key to fetch Beck's wallet from her because she forgot to bring it to her doctor's appointment. She told me it was probably in her bedroom, and when I entered, there were clothes scattered on the floor and drawers half-open. Her wallet was on the bed, somehow easily identifiable amid the chaos. I picked it up and walked to the door, but my foot caught on something, and I fell forward. Getting on my knees, I turned behind me and found a book where my foot had previously been. A vintage hardcover copy of a Kafka book, which surprised me. I never knew Beck was a classics reader.

The spine was loose and worn, and even though I carried it with cupped hands and a faint grasp over to the nightstand, a page fell out anyway. I noticed almost immediately that the colour and paper were different from the ones inside the book, and curiosity ate at me. *Beck won't know if I read it if I put it back*, I had thought. *I'll just peek*. I read the paper, which turned out to be a letter, slowly and then read it again and again. Even though I'd read it multiple times, my whole life changed after reading the first paragraph the first time around.

Beck had lied to me.

Mom didn't kill Randy – Beck did. She shot him with his own gun and Mom took the fall for her. It was accidental, but the outcome was still the same. If she would have only told me, I could have understood. I could have forgiven her. And I could have forgiven our mother, whom I spent a lifetime believing killed her husband with a point-blank shot. But Beck didn't tell me; her sister, her best friend.

The rage that came over me in those moments was unlike anything I'd ever felt before, like weeds growing and spoiling flowers in a garden. I'd clenched my fists so hard that my palms had small, crescent-shaped marks on them days later. I didn't want to be angry at my sister. I wanted to confront her about the letter and give her a chance to explain herself so that we could move on. But after a week went by, my anger deepened. Every time that I would see Beck, or even think of her and what she'd done, my muscles tensed, and my heart beat out of my chest. I started grinding my teeth in my sleep. Eventually, I had to start cutting my fingernails to minimize the damage done to my palms when I'd inevitably dig into them. Beck and I's weekly sister-visits and brunches became a rare occurrence. For a time, I couldn't stand to be near her.

And who could I talk to about this betrayal? No one. Who else knew about the shattered illusions of our shared childhood? My mother and sister; and they've always known. They're the ones who orchestrated I, who kept it from me.. The one person I trusted had betrayed me with a slap to the face. I considered going to visit our mother in prison to get her side of things and ask her, face-to-face. Sure, she may have saved Beck's life by keeping her outside of prison walls, but she robbed me of having a mother. I didn't have a mother to explain having my first period to me or to attend my high school graduation. There were no girls' nights where we sat on the couch for hours on end, watching movies and eating sour candies. No one was there to interrogate Jack Lorelle, the first boy I brought home, or to console me when later that night, he decided we'd be better off as 'just friends.' Sure, Beck was there throughout all those things, and while she did her best to fill the gaping hole in our lives, she could never replace the role of our mother.

As the years went by, I slowly became complacent with the fact that Beck lied to me about the biggest tragedy in our lives. I was able to spend time with her and go on brunch dates, but it never felt quite right. Not on my end, at least.

The door slams shut, and I'm brought back from the depths of my anger. Looking at my phone, I see that forty-five minutes has somehow gone by.

"I'm back!" Beck yells, fumbling with her keys. She kicks her sneakers off and carries the white take-out bags to the kitchen counter.

"I got us pretty much a serving of everything on the menu, but they didn't have any dumplings. Can you believe that? How can a Chinese restaurant be sold out of dumplings? It's tragic." Beck sets the food on the countertop and pretends to dramatically faint.

Beck's careless demeanour and playful tone speak to her cluelessness about my knowledge of her letter. But it's time we finally talk.

"Truly tragic." I smile a half-smile before placing the letter on the countertop, causing Beck to freeze in place.

"Where did you find that?" she finally musters.

"I found it years ago in a book in your room."

"Years?" Beck asks, her voice shrinking. I was almost expecting her to question my being in her room, because she doesn't know if I was snooping or not.

"Years."

"You have to understand, Kins. I was just a kid and – "

"I don't understand *anything* because you've lied to me all these years," I shout. "I was just a kid, too. A kid without a mother or a stable home."

Beck's eyes begin to water but she blinks the tears away. Chester squats at my feet waiting for a scrap of food to drop on the floor so that he can suck it up like a vacuum.

"I was just trying to protect you from carrying the weight of the secret every day. For years, I've had to live with the guilt of not only *killing* someone but also the fact that our mother took the fall for me. I'm an awful person, I know I've done terrible things – but I didn't want you to have to suffer for my sins. I tried so hard to be a mother figure for you, but also a sister and friend. As soon as I was able, I busted my ass working part-time jobs because our living situation was so shitty. We'd already lost our mother, and I know it's selfish, but I guess I didn't want us to lose each other, too."

Somewhere during Beck's speech, something clicks.

We'd already lost our mother.

And she's right. All this time, I didn't stop to consider that for most of the reasons I was angry, Beck had reason to be upset, too. Beck also didn't have a mother figure or anyone to guide her through her teenage years. She had to figure it out herself and then guide me through it.

Beck also lost two parents that night; she witnessed

everything first-hand and was directly traumatized.

I know she lied to me, but now I don't doubt that was her genuine intention. And… things are better this way, aren't they? If Beck hadn't shot Randy, accident or not, he would have kept on abusing us. Who knows what would have happened years down the road? Our mom was never much of an active mother anyway, so I don't think we'd have been better off if Randy were alive. She would have stayed with him until the day she died.

"Say something, *please*," Beck pleads, and I realize I haven't said anything in a minute or two.

Instead of telling Beck any of the thoughts running through my brain, I hug her. She immediately opens her arms and embraces me, and it feels like years since we've had a real hug like this. It probably *has* been years, since everything I've done or said toward my sister has been clouded by buried resentment. But I'm letting go of that anger now – I have to.

"You should mail the letter," I say. Beck releases me from her arms.

"What?"

"I know it was probably more of a diary entry than a real letter meant to be mailed, but I think you should send it to her."

Beck looks wearily at the letter on the kitchen counter.

"I forgive you for lying to me because you were just a

kid, too. None of it was your fault."

The moment the word 'forgive' leaves my mouth, Beck breaks out into tears, and this time it's my turn to comfort her. I bring her into my arms and run my fingers through her auburn hair.

The past six months have been a whirlwind of anger, resentment, and a path toward forgiveness. I've watched Beck struggle through therapy, witnessing her gradual transformation as she confronted the demons that haunted her. When Beck decided to go to therapy and move out of her and Ledger's old apartment, she suggested that we move in together for the time being. And, for one reason or another, I agreed. I think it was because deep inside my being,

Beck eventually stops crying, and we break open the take-out, the clacking of chopsticks against Styrofoam packages filling the room as we consume our Chinese food feast. Beck tells me more about her decision to apply for grad school and her plans to become a psychologist. I tell her I've gone back to work at the coffee shop and have been promoted to shift management, and with it, a whopping 0.95 cent per hour raise. We discuss adopting another dog because Chester is getting up there in age, and we feel like he'd do good with a companion.

In this moment, there is no anger or hurt, and for the first time in ages, I feel like everything is going to be okay

Forty-One

Beck

2019

For the first time in over a decade, I open the letter I wrote to my mother after I killed Randy.

I unfold the crumpled piece of paper with a delicate touch and hold my breath while my hands shake in front of me. I'm held in suspension with my eyes closed for a moment before I open them and read.

DEAR MOM,

I haven't been able to tell anyone anything about that day because I'm scared of what will happen. But because I was scared and didn't tell the truth, you took the blame for me. And I've blamed myself every day since it happened.

I heard the policeman say that the gun had its safety off. I don't know what that means exactly, but I think that it made me able to shoot the gun in the first place. I didn't know how to shoot a gun, so I just took it and squeezed the handle and hoped for the best. If Randy had the safety off then it must have been off for a reason, because that wouldn't have been safe to walk around with it off. Maybe that's why they call it the gun's safety. But Randy was as stupid as he was mean so it wouldn't surprise me one bit if he did walk around with it off.

I'm sorry. I keep forgetting that he was your husband. I don't know why you married him but it was the worst decision you could have possibly made. Why would you marry him when you could have done so much better?

Or not marry anyone at all?

Sometimes I hated you because you brought him into our lives. But then I'd remember that he hurt you worse than me or Kinsley. How did you stay with him after he hit you for the first time? You must have known he hurt us too because I always had bruises, but they were on my shoulders so that no one else could see them unless I wore a sleeveless shirt, so maybe you didn't know. I like to believe you didn't know. He treated Kinsley bad too and made fun of her all the time because she has trouble reading and is shy. I thought you must have been blind or heartless, but I guess I'm heartless too because I killed a man. Even if it was an accident and if even if he was a monster who hurt my family, I still killed someone. And even worse, someone I love took the blame for it.

You don't deserve to live the rest of your life in prison. Kinsley doesn't deserve to suffer from my mistake, either. She's innocent in all of this and had her mom taken from her. At least if I had gotten caught then they would have gone easier on me since I'm young. I could have gone to that prison for children or something. But they won't go easy on you. Now you won't go to Kinsley's graduation or get to see her get married or anything. You won't see me do any of that either, but like I said, I don't deserve it. I'm the one who did the bad thing. It should be me behind bars.

It's been 12 days since you were taken away and Kinsley hasn't stopped crying the whole time. I'm sad too. We've been staying with Aunt Bee, but I don't think she's happy to have us, which makes me sadder. I hope Kinsley and I can stay here with Aunt Bee and our cousins. They're the only family we have left. It was you and me and Kinsley for a long time and things were great. But then you had to go and marry Randy and ruin it all. I feel bad saying that but it's true. I'm glad he's gone, but I wish you didn't have to go away. It isn't fair.

I think you thought the best chance at repairing the heart of our family was to go away to my place so I could have a childhood, but really, you made it worse for Kinsley. She needs her mom, but I'll step in. I promise I'll take care of her no matter what.

Kinsley doesn't really understand what happened.

That's a good thing, I think. She believes what you told everyone, which is that you killed Randy. She doesn't understand how her mom could do something so bad like that. I'm afraid of the day she finds out what really happened with you and me and Randy. She may never speak to me again, so maybe I won't ever tell her. That's all too far in the future anyway. I can't even picture what I'm doing tomorrow, let alone ten years from now.

Maybe you'll be done prison in ten years and will be home with us again. I know we don't go to church, but I think I'll start praying to God that you get out of jail soon. He must know that it wasn't you who killed Randy, so he'll help you out. I'll say my first prayer tonight and I'll tell him I say hi to Grandma and Grandpa, too.

I don't know if I'll ever send this letter to you. I don't know where to send a jail letter, either. But I'm writing a letter because there's too much going on inside my head. I've been so angry and sad and frustrated that I just want to scream. Sometimes I do scream into my pillow and cry at the same time. I hate everything. I hate myself for what I did. And I hate that you protected me from what happened next. The guilt is eating me alive. Maybe I deserve to be eaten by it.

I'm sorry for everything. I love you.

LOVE BECK

I fold the paper back to the way it was before, the secrets and memories of a younger me settled deep within its creases.

Instead of going into a book or a shoebox, I place the piece of paper into a cream envelope. My taste buds register a faint taste of adhesive as I lick the seal of the fresh envelope and press the middle with my thumb. I place a stamp with the Canadian flag on the top right corner and double-check that the address of the prison is correct. Then, I make the two-minute walk from my new apartment to the community mailbox drop-off to mail the letter.

The crisp autumn air cools my face, the city coated in hues of yellow and auburn and orange. When I arrive at the box and pull the little metal door open, I carefully place the envelope inside, my hand lingering on the handle before I let go.

Let go of the letter – and the anger and guilt it represents.

Without Kinsley forgiving me and suggesting I send the letter, I don't think I ever would have mailed it. I'm not sending the letter to hurt my mom, even though that might have been one of my initial intentions in writing it. My mom was a victim, just like Kinsley and I were, and I was too young at the time and too stubborn all these years later to accept that. She was probably torn between her love and duty as a mother, and the fear of what might happen if she tried to leave Randy. And yet, despite the constant acts of violence and the emotional toll it took on all of us, she stayed. I didn't understand her decision. Hell, for years I resented the choices she made. But going to therapy these past few months has helped me come to terms with different responses and coping mechanisms of abuse victims. It's also helped me relate to my mom by accepting that my relationship with Ledger was toxic and emotionally abusive. This common ground has finally helped me reach a point where I can forgive both my mom and me and exorcize the ghosts of my past.

My therapist, Dr. Goode, says that everyone has 'ghosts'. He describes them as shadows, calling out from the darkest corners of your mind because they've been buried for so long. Ghosts are the scars that never quite fade, the wounds that never quite heal, and the regrets that never quite go away. And Dr. Goode has helped me realize that eliminating those ghosts isn't about expunging the mistakes I've made or disregarding my suffering; it's about acknowledging and accepting my past and learning to coexist with it in a way that allows me to move forward.

And I have – moved forward, that is.

I recently moved out of my and Ledger's apartment and moved into a loft that I share with Kinsley and her dog, Chester. After Kinsley was cleared of her charges and returned home to Ontario, she was ecstatic to discover that Chester survived the Mull House Massacre, but she wasn't thrilled that he'd been in a kennel, on hold, for so long. Soon after my visit with Sam, I contacted the kennel in Nova Scotia and explained our situation, and after yet another trip out East, I was allowed to take Chester home with me. I took care of him until Kinsley, too, came home.

Despite being adamant about not wanting a student loan before, I decided to apply for grad school at UofT anyways. My desire for a debt-free education was one of the largest reasons I joined The Larua Group, and the biggest motivator behind the Mull House job. And although I wish the Mull House incident never happened and that no one had to die, for my own sanity, I need to give myself some semblance of meaning to the tragedy. So, after going to therapy and clearing my head, I gave my trauma meaning through action: I'm pursuing my dream anyway. My very expensive, financially exhausting, dream. I'll eventually be able to pay off the debts after I graduate and get a position as a psychologist or therapist, even if it takes years and multiple loans. I want to be in a position to help people get through their own traumas and heal, and psychology is how I'll do that.

Kinsley is in the clear and on her own healing journey. She feels guilty about colluding with Linda, but I was never mad at her for it. She did what she did out of guilt and a desire to help someone she'd hurt. When it came down to it, and Linda went rogue from their plan, Kinsley protected me and saved my life. She didn't know about Linda's ulterior motives and desire to take out the entirety of The Larua Group, so how can I blame her? My willingness to forgive so readily does nothing to aid her own guilt, though. No matter how much I assure her that it's fine, that *we're* fine, her guilt continues to follow her. At least Chester helps where I fall short.

Chester acts as Kinsley's unofficial therapy dog and calms both of us down if we get anxious or have a nightmare. That wrinkled munchkin is more help than I ever gave him credit for – Chester, the forgotten survivor of Mull House.

Sam still mourns Toby's death but honours his memory in everything he does. He's started wearing both wedding bands on his ring finger, and when he first showed me, I cried. They'd bought the set of traditional, golden bands, but never got the chance to share their vows and join their lives together. My heart breaks for Sam, he and Toby were so in love. I'm not sure if he'll ever move on and find someone else, but I hope he'll find love again one day. He deserves to be happy, and although I'd only just gotten to know him, I'd like to think Toby would want Sam to be happy, too.

When I'm ready, I hope I'll find love one day, too. Real love, not the bullshit I had with Ledger. Sometimes I catch myself thinking about him, missing him. But I quickly remind myself that he wasn't good for me or to me, that our relationship wasn't healthy. I've vowed to never become involved with anyone who treats me with a *lesser than thou* attitude, and I'll wait however long it takes for that person to come into my life; I won't settle. For now, though, I'm content working on myself and towards earning my degree.

I've served other people my entire life – it's time to just focus on Beck.

My past may be murky and littered with skeletons and ghosts, with black and grey morality, but the path to my future is clear as day. The shadows of Randy and the Carlsons and Mull House still linger, and they probably always will, but they will no longer define me. Every step I take will bring me closer to the life I envision, the goals I chase, and the person I aspire to be.

Epilogue

Beck

2027

"It's been haunting me, and I can't seem to shake it off."

My patient, Lorelei Vasquez, sits across from me on my office's loveseat, her legs bouncing with fervour.

"I'm here to listen, Lorelei. Remember, this is a safe space," I reassure her.

"I've talked to you about it before, so this isn't new. But it's just this… fear I have of drowning. It's consuming all of my thoughts and impacting every aspect of my life. I can't do the dishes or watch my son at his swimming lessons. The mere thought of water terrifies me, and it feels like I'm drowning even when I'm not near any water, to begin with. This – this feeling of being trapped is so helpless and suffocating, and it follows me everywhere I go."

Lorelei's eyes redden and glaze over with tears, so I offer her a tissue, and she accepts it with a shaky hand. I refrain from pointing out that the tears coming out of her eyes are water, too.

"I'm sorry to hear about this, Lorelei. It sounds like this fear is a lot more pervasive than when we last met with each other, and that's not the direction we want to be headed in. I understand that this fear is causing you a great deal of distress, so let's explore it a bit further, shall we? Have you noticed any specific triggers or incidents that might be linked to this fear?"

The alarm I set for sixty minutes chimes from my phone, and I try not to look disappointed. This is the worst part of my job, the fact that there's a time limit on how much I can directly help people in one session.

"Lorelei, your bravery and determination to overcome your fear are truly admirable, and I'll be here with you every step of the way, for as long as you'll have me. And if you'd like, you can book your next appointment with the front desk on the way out."

I wave her off and sink back into my black leather chair to enjoy a moment's peace. The landline on my desk rings, and there goes the peace and quiet. I suppose that's to be expected when my profession is quite literally talking, though.

"Your 11:00 am is running a bit late, Rebecca."

"Okay, thanks for letting me know, Sheila."

I hang up the receiver and thank God for giving me my super-human receptionist and friend, Sheila. She's been a lifesaver since I opened my own clinical psychology practice last year. I'm still a relatively new psychologist, but we've been networking and have grown our clientele quickly. I couldn't have done any of it without her, or without my husband, Marcus. Marcus's family comes from money, and he was adamant about helping fund the start-up costs for my dream of opening a practice. I was hesitant and stubborn at first, but I'm learning to take help when I need it. He wanted to help pay off my student loans too, but I refused that offer – there's a limit to my growth.

I smile thinking about Marcus and decide to take the opportunity to check in with him, even though it's only been a few hours since I've left home.

"Hey, sweetie, what's going on?" Marcus says. We've been married for five years now, and he still calls me pet names, which I think is romantic. I never thought I was the hopeless romantic type until I met my husband, and he changed everything I thought I knew about love.

"Hey, nothing much. I've just got a couple of extra minutes in between appointments this morning and thought I'd give you a call to see how things are going at home."

Rustling sounds come through the phone in response.

"I think someone wants to talk to you," Marcus says, laughing.

"Mommy!" our three-year-old daughter, Paige, says.

"Are you being a good girl for Daddy?" I ask in a faux-authoritative tone. It's so hard to be serious with her, and for better or worse, Marcus and I both spoil her rotten. "Because Daddy told me we could go out for ice cream tonight after dinner… but only if you don't get into any trouble. Can you do that for Mommy and Daddy?"

"I want ice cream!" she squeals. "Bye, Mommy. Luh you!"

"I love you!"

Paige hangs up the phone before passing it back to her father, and I laugh. Instead of calling back, I send Marcus a text telling him I'll call again when I'm on my way home tonight. I usually finish the workday around 6:00 pm, but on Fridays, I get off early, so I'll be out of here by 5:00 pm at the latest.

My heart swells with pride and affection at this beautiful little human, half me and half the man I love. There was a time when I never thought I'd find love, real love, again. But after going to therapy and discussing my relationship with Ledger, among other things, I was in the right headspace to pursue Marcus's romantic advances when we met at UofT.

Kinsley is expecting a little boy any day now, so Paige will have a cousin and playmate soon, too. We don't plan on having another baby for another few years, so we'll live vicariously through Kinsley and her baby for the time being. She's over nearly every day anyway, so we'll be seeing plenty of baby Rollins.

There's a knock at my office door, signalling the arrival of my late-11:00 am patient.

I already read her intake file this morning when I got into the office. Her name is Charlie Carlton, but she prefers to go by CeCe. She's young, only fifteen years old, and although this will be her first session with me, she's no stranger to therapy. By the looks of it, she's gone therapist/psychologist/psychiatrist shopping frequently over the last year, trading in each one after a few sessions.

Maybe I'll be the one to make a real difference in her life. Cases like these, ones with children, are what really inspired me to do this career in the first place.

"Hi, please take a seat wherever you feel comfortable."

CeCe wanders in, the array of framed diplomas hanging

on the opposite wall immediately catching her eye.

"You can just call me Rebecca if you'd like," I say, smiling so that she won't feel intimidated.

"Okay."

"So, CeCe, what brings you into my office?"

I already know about her abandonment issues and depressive episodes via her intake form, filled out by her parents, but it's important to build rapport with my clients.

"When I get overwhelmed, this crazy side of me takes over. It's like a fire inside me that I can't control. And because I'm always so overwhelmed and angry, I end up pushing people away, even those who care about me. The sadness that comes with that hits hard. I feel empty, alone, angry."

"Those feelings of anger and sadness can really weigh someone down, especially a teenager such as yourself. But I want you to know that we're here to work through it together. I'm not sure how your previous therapists have done things, but in my office, we're a team – we have a partnership. And hopefully, therapy can help you understand the root of these emotions and find healthier ways to cope. How does that sound?"

"I'm tired of feeling like this all the time. I want to trust people and have better relationships." She ignores my question entirely and I take a moment to inventory the situation.

CeCe's posture is stiff, her hands made into tight fists

that are crossed in her lap. She has a general lack of facial expression, but that could be because of her clenched jaw. Her blonde hair is artfully styled into a French braid, and she's wearing a light layer of makeup. She takes care of herself, which contradicts the intake form that claims she's too depressed to shower or brush her teeth, let alone do makeup. This could only be because it's her first meeting with a new therapist, though.

"I understand, CeCe. It takes courage to reach out for help, and I'm so glad you've come here, to my office. Our goal is to support you in navigating your abandonment issues, managing anger, and finding ways to improve your mental well-being."

"I didn't say anything to you about abandonment."

Shit shit shit. How could I be so careless?

"You're right, I'm sorry. It was on your intake form, and I thought –"

"That form is a load of bull. It's fiction."

"Sorry, could you elaborate on that?" I plaster a smile on my face to keep the façade of composure, but my stomach is on a rollercoaster.

"I must have given you the wrong form. I'm so sorry. Let me fix that for you."

For the first time since stepping into my office, CeCe smiles. She digs into her tote bag and retrieves yet another intake form. She hands it to me, and I can't do anything to hide the sight of my jaw dropping to the floor.

NEW PATIENT INTAKE QUESTIONNAIRE

Date: April 6th, 2027

Name:

Charlie (Charlotte) Carlson

Age and DOB:

15 y/o; October 8th, 2012

Gender:

Cis. Female

Family history of mental illness, if applicable:

Father a presumed schizophrenic; manic depression in
Mother

Marital and familial status:

Single; Mother – dead. Father – dead. Older brother –
dead. Middle older brother – dead. Grandparents –
dead.

I close my eyes, not able to continue reading the form. This cannot be happening.

"Cat got your tongue?" CeCe, *Charlotte*, says. "What's the matter, you can't treat me, Beck? I'm your patient, after all."

"I actually go by Rebecca in my professional field," I correct gently.

"But this isn't professional, though, is it? This is as personal as it gets."

"Charlotte, whatever you've heard about me and your family, I can explain."

"Shut up," she snaps. For privacy reasons, the walls of my office are sound-proofed, so Sheila won't hear the yelling come from inside the room or any call for help I might want to make.

"I don't remember much about when my dad and brothers were killed. I was only four or five. But I remember the aftermath, and in the short time we spent together after their deaths, my mother was too depressed to bathe me or herself. Most days, I didn't have one meal, let alone three. I had to borrow snacks from classmates who bullied me. I grew up with a mom who was there but not *there*, only for her to be taken away from me, too. Do you know how hard it is to be orphaned before you reach double freaking digits?"

"Look, I'm so sorry about your family, Charlotte, I really am. I grew up without a mom, too, so I know how difficult that can be."

"Except your mom isn't dead. You can still call up your mom in prison, but mine is dead. She died in your place, and it was your bitch sister who killed her. It should have been *you!*"

Charlotte pulls out something else from her bag and my body recoils, fearing the worst. Instead of a gun or knife, she retrieves her cell phone and checks the time.

"It looks like our time is up."

"What did you come here for Charlotte?" I ask hesitantly; the second shoe has yet to drop, and I'm bracing myself. "Did you just need to get these things off your chest? Do you need help?

"I didn't come here to get anything other than your time and attention." Charlotte picks up her tote bag and turns to leave my office.

"Wait," I shout after her. "What does that mean?"

"Thanks for talking with me, Beck. I feel so much better already. Be careful out there today. They say it's going to be scorching hot."

She leaves, and my mind draws a blank.

And then it clicks.

I run out of my office, Charlotte already far out of my

sight. Sheila stands up at her desk as I sprint by, but she never gets a chance to inquire about what the hell is going on. Even I don't know what the hell is going on, but I have a suspicion. But I don't want to be right; I can't be right, not about this.

On the way home, I drive at least 30km over the speed limit and call the police on my phone. My body jerks with the car as I cut the wheel, avoiding a collision after drifting into the left lane. I'm breaking just about every rule they teach in driver's ed.

I tell the police that I need all emergency services at my house.

"What is the emergency, ma'am?" the operator asks.

"I'm fearing for my life and for my family. I think one of my patients – I'm a psychologist – might be on her way to my home to do something bad. She's going to do something; I can feel it in my bones."

I try calling Marcus on his cell, but it goes straight to voicemail. I throw my phone on the passenger's side floor in frustration.

I turn the corner like a racing car in the grand prix and pull into the driveway, but there are several vehicles already occupying its space: a police car, two ambulances… and Kinsley's blue sedan.

She must have come to visit Marcus and Paige while I was at work. She does that sometimes because she's that good of a sister.

No no no.

A fire truck sits parked along the curb, its ladder completely extended and angled toward my house. My house, which is engulfed in flames. I haphazardly park my car at the foot of the driveway and swing the driver's side door open.

The moment I'm outside, the acrid scent of smoke fills my body, stinging my nostrils and threatening to steal away my breath. Despite this, I run towards my home, but am held back by two police officers.

"Ma'am, there is an active fire. I can't allow you to be on the premises," he tells me calmly. How the hell is he so calm?

"This is my house," I yell, waving my hands. "My family is inside. You have to save them, please."

There's a loud noise, and I see that one of the windows in the living room has exploded, shattered glass littering the ground outside. The police officer escorts me away from the house and hands me off to a paramedic; they make me sit in the back of the ambulance, its doors perched open. They tell me the fire will be out soon, but it does nothing to ease my mind. I need to see that Marcus and Paige and Kinsley are all right.

As I sit in the ambulance, I hear whispers of an 'explosive device' and 'arson' and 'foul play'. I wait to hear the words 'no fatalities' but they never come.

The weight of anticipation hangs heavy in the hazy, humid air, mingling with a sense of impending doom. A prayer forms on my lips as I say their names, willing the universe to hear my desperate plea. *Marcus, Paige, Kinsley; Marcus, Paige, Kinsley.* But the fire and wailing sirens swallow my words whole, leaving only whispers in their wake. They're trapped inside that inferno, their lives hanging in the balance as I'm being rescued. My soul shatters at the realization, splintering into countless shards of grief.

That's when I'm shooed out of the ambulance and see the first body bag come out of my house. I choke on a scream that never leaves my mouth and collapse on the ground. Paramedics load the bag into an ambulance, the one I was sitting in just moments before. Before I even have time to think or breathe, a second bag is carried out of the house, this one much smaller. Tears blur my vision and I vomit on the grass, kneeling over into my own bile. Forehead pressed to the ground, I hear the ambulance doors shut with a *thud* and the sound of tires on gravel. But then I hear the sound of wheels squeaking on the pavement, and when I finally muster the strength to look up, I see someone being pushed into the back of the second ambulance - and they're not in a body bag.

I'm too tired to even question who the third person is because my husband is gone and so is my daughter and our home. My entire life, and theirs, snuffed out like a flame. I begin to sob uncontrollably, the floodgates bursting open. I fear I'll never be able to close them again.

"Miss, can you come with us for a moment?" a voice asks.

"Huh?" I mumble.

"Quick, before the ambulance leaves."

A female paramedic helps me off the ground and rushes me over to the remaining ambulance, where I see Kinsley strapped into the gurney wearing an oxygen mask.

We make eye contact, and then the doors are slammed shut. The ambulance wastes no time in speeding away, its sirens flashing and echoing through the streets.

Police officers begin to walk over to me, and they're asking questions. But all I can do is stare at the empty husk that is my house. It's burnt to a crisp, and so is everything inside it. I don't know how I'll go on, or if I even want to live without my family. I don't know whether Kinsley will survive, either. But I do know that no matter what happens next, my heart will be forever scorched by the searing grip of loss.

The End

***

Please consider leaving a review or rating for this

book. It helps us authors out a lot!

Acknowledgements

It is mind-boggling to be writing the acknowledgements for my sophomore novel, *The Clearing*.

For *The Clearing*, I wanted to challenge myself and do something different; I wanted to bend genres. My book is a suspense novel that toys with the idea of supernaturalism, only for the paranormal aspects to prove false and ultimately aid in the thrilling twists and turns. For this project, I also challenged myself to work more on my character development, and although it may not be perfect, I am proud of how much I have grown as a writer in this publication compared to my earlier works. I hope to continue growing professionally and personally with each following book I write & publish.

The general setting in which some of the novel takes place is based on a real town called Mulgrave, situated near Cape Breton Island in the province of Nova Scotia, Canada. It is the town from which my family hails, and many of my extended family members still reside there. Over the span of my life, I have found a second home in Mulgrave and wanted to share that love in my book. The name of Mull House is also an homage to the town's name. During Summer visits, family and family friends (and friends of friends) have been incredibly supportive of my first two books, *Bird Boy* and *I Did It For You*. Thank you to Mulgrave and its residents for providing me with a home away from home, and a home for my story.

Since I thanked you last in my previous book, I think I will bump you up for *The Clearing*. Thank you to my partner, Ethan, for being so supportive of my passion and continuing to tolerate my creative tirades and 4:00 am writing nights. I hope you know that you have years of these tirades and tireless nights to (not) look forward to.

Thank you to my parents for your continued support

of me and my authoring career. I take pride in knowing you approve of my passion and are proud of my accomplishments. Dad, I know the dad-ager gig does not pay much, but maybe there will be a raise in the future.

Thanks to Claire, my best friend, who is also and the editor of *The Clearing*. I hold you, your opinions, and your expertise in such high regard, and I wouldn't trust anyone else to edit my book.

A big thank you goes to my amazing management team and coworkers at the Oshawa Centre Indigo. Thank you for being supportive and encouraging me to get myself out there. I never would have been so confident at my first book signing in July 2022 if it were not for them. They hosted me at the store, giving me a familiar environment to do something that was previously uncomfortable for me. As of 2023, I have quite a few events, signings, and readings under my belt, and I credit my confidence to that very first book signing at Indigo Oshawa. Thank you for your continued support. A special shout-out goes to Ally for being my friend, beta reader, creative advisor, and confidant in all things writing.

Finally, thank you to you, the reader! I would not be where I am today without you, and your support truly means the world to me. I hope you join me for the next release, and stay tuned because this isn't the last you've heard of *The Clearing* universe…

The 'Real' Mull House

It goes without saying that nearly everything in my suspense novel, *The Clearing*, is fictional.

However, during a visit to Nova Scotia in 2022, I came across a gorgeous house just outside of Mulgrave, in Guysborough. The building captivated me! It was old and grand and unlike anything I had ever seen before in person. After doing some research, I discovered that this house is historically known as Maguire Mansion and was built sometime in the 19th century. Some residents nearby expressed that there was an urban legend of sorts about the mansion. Some even believed it to be haunted. There were also rumours that the body of an infant was discovered hidden in between the walls of the house…

Regardless of whether or not these tales hold any truth, they are what first gave me the inspiration to write this story.

Full disclosure, though; I have never been inside of Maguire Mansion and have only ever seen photos, which vastly differ from *The Clearing*'s Mull House. In my book, all the interior of the house and some of the exterior is fictive or exaggerated in one way or another.

Please note, I have immense respect for this historic landmark and do not mean any harm by using it as inspiration for my novel.

About the author:

Jordan Murray is the author of *The Clearing*, *I Did It For You*, and *Bird Boy: and Other Short Stories*. Originally born in Toronto, Canada, she lives in Ontario suburbia with her many, many books.

Jordan has a BA honours degree in English literature, and she also works part-time at her favorite bookstore. She is studying to become a primary teacher. When she isn't writing, Jordan is reading; when she isn't reading, she is buying and collecting books. Good for the soul, debilitating for the wallet. At least there's the employee discount!

Follow Jordan's Instagram and TikTok accounts for book

reviews and writing updates (@lovelyliterary). Visit her official

author webstore to purchase signed copies of her books.

www.ingramcontent.com/pod-product-compliance
Lightning Source LLC
Chambersburg PA
CBHW051124190726
48290CB00006B/1683